# The Lord's Son

Jack Holbrook

Irish Creek Publishing


Cover illustration: Jim Theodore Studio


ISBN: 0615894461
ISBN-13: 978-0615894461

# DEDICATION

I want to thank my father and mother, John and Lucile, for
providing me with a wonderful spiritual heritage. And my wife,
Betsy, for her love and tireless support of my writing. Finally, I
want to thank our children, Judith, Katherine, Jonathan, and
Peter, for joining me in my love of stories.

# CONTENTS

# Chapter 1

## THE NIGHT OF THE DRAGON

There was a dragon in Edenton, so to Edenton I ran—through ancient forests, over moonlit meadows, down misty creek beds. Past the dead of night, I ran. Past a stag fleeing hungry wolves, past a fox's retreat from the sudden breeze, past the rushing wings of an owl; come wooded hill, come steaming pond, come brush and bog—over all I ran. Yet I breathed the dewy air with strength to spare, for I ran in the name of my Captain, He who leads angel armies.

There was a dragon in Edenton, so to Edenton I ran.

Edenton, a quiet Wessex village, was surrounded by ancient forests of oak and beech. The land was owned by Lord Erlan. The men of the village worked for Erlan just as their fathers had worked for Erlan's father. It was an orderly and peaceful village till the dragon came.

The gloomy village, lit by a few fires and candlelight glowing from cottages, came into view. "Halt!" came a shout from the darkness before me. I stopped running and watched as someone stepped from behind a tree. He was of angel kind, yet the light of my Captain's glory no longer shone from him. He was a fallen angel with eyes dark, sunken, and lifeless. "Turn back!" the fallen one cried with sword upraised. "None may enter Edenton tonight by orders of the great dragon!"

Something familiar I saw in this fallen one. I drew my sword slowly. "Zorran?" I asked.

"I am Bittenrood. Zorran was my name before we won our independence."

"Do you not remember me?"

"I remember you."

I placed my sword back in its scabbard. "I've no desire to fight you or send you to hell. Let me pass. You know I must fulfill my mission."

Bittenrood lowered his sword. "Hell is pain beyond imagining," he said quietly. "But I cannot let you enter Edenton tonight. Dragon is angry and orders have been given…and if I'm caught disobeying…."

"I must go."

"No! You can choose to turn away just like we who've fallen from heavens' realms. We do not follow like blind fools. Nor should you. Make your choice. Turn away and take your freedom!"

He glared at me, and I at him: faithful angel and fallen one. Both of us willful, but he filled with anger at all things good— all things reminding him of his former captain.

Said I to him, "You are right. I must make a choice. I choose to go to Edenton."

I took a step toward Edenton. "I choose to go," I repeated firmly with my eyes fixed on Bittenrood's dark face.

A fallen angel's mind is hard to know for the sunken eyes reveal little, but I thought there was sadness in the creature. For the moment, his anger seemed to have faded. As I turned toward Edenton, I wondered if I might have seen a flicker of light in the dark eyes. But I dared not look back, lest he change his mind and attack; fallen angels rarely show mercy. Not only are they filled with hatred and anger—they also fear their master's wrath.

Angels, fallen or faithful, are eternal; they cannot die. But, in battle, angels may receive wounds that fell them. Injured angels are taken from this earth for restoration. Faithful angels are taken to heaven. Fallen angels are gathered up by demonic "seekers" and taken to the nether region called hell—the one place in this universe where God has withdrawn His presence and there dwells nothing good; even the devils scarcely speak of it. The hellish effect is to "restore" the body while the hideous darkness of the place produces a more evil creature than before. Several trips to the place and all traces of an angel's form are gone; what is left is no more than a devil.

Now at the last moment when I had begun to think that Bittenrood would not attack, he shouted, "Stay!" I whirled about, drawing my sword. Bittenrood furiously swung his two-edged sword at me. I drew myself up and blocked the blow. He struck again and again with a power borne out of desperate anger. He was relentless, and it took all of my strength to block the blows.

But the ferocity of the attack did not last. The blows came slower and with less force. His fury faded, giving me time to collect myself and watch for an unguarded move. A moment later the opportunity came. Bittenrood swung a little too high and missed me altogether. I dodged the blow rather than blocking it and swung my sword into the opening, catching him in the chest. Bittenrood's sword slipped from his hand. He fell backward and lay still upon the ground. I knelt over him. He gazed up at me for only a second with blank, lifeless eyes. Then a look of fear crossed his face, and he moved no more.

I wept over him. In his face, I saw the faded lines of a once glorious creature. Though he could no longer hear me, I said, "With grief I raised my sword against you, Zorran. The day now past when you forsook the favor of our Captain, pursuing glory that would be your own. This lie has made you its slave; freedom comes from the Creator alone."

I sensed something in the darkness behind me. There was a fluttering sound to my left—a quick, dark movement, and it was gone.

*We were being watched*, I realized. *If Zorran had not attacked, he would have been punished for showing mercy and failing to fight.*

As I turned away, I was reminded of something I have heard angels say, "Those who have rebelled long so for mercy that they occasionally show it themselves just to know it again."

Edenton was hushed, though the stillness was not that of a peacefully sleeping village. I could hear things creeping through the dark. Spirits moved about in the shadows like dogs, nervous before a storm. *Where is Dragon?* I wondered.

Dragons are spirits that find their life in the darkness of a human heart—a heart that has allowed bitterness, anger, or jealousy to creep in becomes a dragon's home. As the evil grows, so does the power of the dragon. Edenton's dragon found its home in the heart of Acwellen, the husband of Lord Erlan's wife's sister.

Gabriel, archangel of earth, sent me to Edenton to help Zophar, the angel guardian of the village. Until recently, Zophar stood watch over the orbit of planets at the far reaches of the universe. But he became restless and requested a different mission, so Gabriel placed him over Edenton. All went well till Dragon arrived. When Gabriel heard about Dragon, he decided that Zophar would need help. So he sent me to oversee Edenton's battle for freedom and help Zophar learn the ways of mankind on the earth.

I entered the village on the northeast side, near the road to Iconium. I saw there an angel standing alone. Like me, he was one half taller than the tallest man. But he was broader than I and stood as strong as an oak tree. His long red hair made him appear as if his head and neck were on fire. His face seemed locked in an eternal frown till he saw me—then it faded for a moment.

"Iothiel?"

"Greetings, Zophar. Blessings to you from Gabriel."

The frown returned to his face, and he nodded. "Fierce is the air in this village. The angels and demons will fight when Erlan returns."

"When will Erlan come?"

"He and his thane have ridden this way all day. Any moment they could appear on the road," Zophar replied. "Meanwhile, Acwellen and Gwendolyn have set a trap. When

Erlan arrives, he will face Acwellen and twenty hired swordsmen; all thieves and scoundrels. Lady Cwen is near childbirth and does not know what is about to take place. Dragon has made himself powerful in Acwellen."

Zophar paused. "Did Gabriel speak to you about this matter? What says he?

"He says," I replied quietly, "we are not to intervene in this fight."

Zophar stared at me in disbelief. "What? Not intervene?"

I shook my head.

"Is there nothing we can do?" Zophar cried. "Erlan and his entire household will be killed."

"At least one shall not be killed. While Dragon is intent on Erlan, you and I are to snatch a seed from Dragon's claws."

Zophar placed his hand on his sword hilt. "When devils attacked the orbit of the planets, we fought them off with the sword. Why can we not do that here?"

I looked hard at Zophar. I had assumed that he understood the difference between guarding planets and guarding mankind.

"Devils may try to disrupt the orbit of planets to disorder the Creator's cosmos. But men, weak as they are, have a will and are made in the image of the Creator. In guarding mankind, we must be careful not to violate their will or ignore the Creator's plan, no matter how trying it may be. For it is this weakness of men and the glory given them by the Creator that tries the patience of angels and causes devils to make war upon them."

I continued, "The Creator takes greater delight in the faith of these mortals who stand fast regardless of their plight, than He takes in the strength of angel armies. We take part in this plan merely as guardians of man."

"As I am charged with guarding Erlan and this village," he swore, "how can you forbid me to draw my sword upon the enemy?"

"Was it not Erlan who allowed Acwellen to gain power in the manor? Had he been more diligent, would he not have seen his brother-in-law's growing resentment and anger that has fed Dragon?"

Zophar sighed and glanced about the silent cottages. "I did not suspect how deeply the devils' rebellion runs through each man and woman, there is the spark of glory in some of them, but to see a man plot the death of his own kinsman; I could not have imagined it."

Zophar looked at me, but I made no reply. We both knew evil had begun with the angels and had spread to man. And it brought us no joy to see what pain it effected on each man, woman, and child, spreading like ripples on a pond.

"Your time of guarding Erlan is ending. You and I shall be guarding someone new. Our mission's success depends greatly upon him."

Just then a shuffling came from the gate. The bulky form of the butcher appeared and plodded through the trees. A small black-winged devil rode on his back, whispering in the portly man's ear. Zophar pulled his sword from its sheath and stung the unsuspecting devil in the side. It fell from the man's back and disappeared into the night. The butcher shrieked and fell over, shivering in fear. "Who's there? Who's there?" he cried.

"Hold your sword," I told Zophar. "Behold, Erlan and his thane, Bors, approach."

* * *

That same night in Edenton, there was a smith whose wife was giving birth to a child. She had lain in bed all day. In the evening she began to moan and weep and call for help. The smith, to whom she had promised a boy to help him in the shop, hurried down the street to fetch the midwife.

"She'll not be here," the midwife's husband said. "She's gone to the manor house to deliver Lady Cwen's child and hasn't returned."

The smith knocked at the tanner's door. "My wife's time has come," he said. "The midwife be with Lady Cwen. Your wife has borne five children. Please send her to help my wife."

The tanner's wife came. About midnight, a newborn baby boy began to cry in the smith's house. The tanner's wife left, and the smith smiled at the tiny boy. He rubbed the little hands, willing them to grow big and strong and hold hammers and tongs.

The smith's wife nursed the baby while her husband lay down to a contented sleep. But just as he began to snore, he was aroused by a pounding at his door.

"Ormod! Wake up, Ormod!"

The smith rose from his bed and stumbled to the door. He opened it to find the midwife holding a tiny bundle. She held it out to him.

"Ormod, your wife is having a child; take this one too. She can nurse it with the other and you can tell people you had twins. See, 'tis a boy. He can help in your shop."

Ormod looked at the bundle and shook his head. "But we have a baby boy."

"Then your wife can nurse this one next to it. Here!" she said forcing it into his arms.

"But where does it come from?"

"Do not ask that, Ormod. You are the child's only hope. If anyone asks questions, tell them you had twin boys. Care for the child as your own!"

A cold rain had begun, so the midwife pulled her hood over her head as she hurried away. Behind her the bewildered smith stood holding the tiny baby in his thick, hairy arms.

# Chapter 2

## THE FESTIVAL

Zophar led me through Edenton; past the villagers' little wood and mud cottages, past the smith shop, and past the carpenter shop. All around us, people milled about the booths set up for the May Day festival or, as the villagers called it, "fetching in the May." Angels stood guard over the faithful and a few not so faithful. Devils tended to those who believed in only what they could see, for these people were easier to lead astray. Zophar pointed the way through the booths toward the manor house lawn.

"The passing of winters has reached seventeen, Iothiel."

I knew very well how many years it had been and what he was referring to, but I said, "You speak of winters passing since Acwellen killed Erlan, and Dragon has ruled Edenton?"

"And every year Acwellen takes more barley from the villagers' fields," he went on, "more bread from the miller, more from the smith, the carpenter...." Zophar glanced back to see if I was listening.

The last half year I spent in the land of Hibernia, fighting devils from across the northern sea. Upon my return, Zophar met me on the north edge of the village. It appeared to me that the village was little changed, but Zophar guided me through the streets as if it were my first visit to Edenton since Dragon came.

"How much change does a planet go through in seventeen years?" I asked.

"Planets and people are not the same thing. Acwellen has grown bolder, and Dragon has grown stronger."

We passed the Maypole, an evergreen tree shorn of its branches, around which girls with flowers in their hair would dance. In the time before Lord Erlan, May Day festivals had been a pagan affair with lewd and vulgar acts and was the delight of devils. But when the message of the humble Christ came to Edenton and the surrounding villages all that changed. The May Day festival became an innocent celebration with children singing, dancing, and wearing flowers. To join in the festivities, shopkeepers and craftsmen from local villages set up booths to sell their wares.

Zophar stopped and pointed to a platform being built next to the Maypole. "See? A stage is set—a stage for one man to watch another die."

"A contest unto death?"

Zophar nodded. "The rules defined by Acwellen are thus—any prisoner may challenge another prisoner. The one who challenges gets to choose the weapons."

"Like the Roman contests under Marcus Aurelius," I said.

"The gladiators?"

"Over five hundred years ago, when you were guarding planets, I was in Rome where the gladiators fought to the death. I suspect Dragon was in Rome as well."

Zophar scowled. "Since the day Acwellen killed Erlan, Edenton has grown ever more evil. Erlan's son is now a young man toiling in the smith shop, no more ready to contest Dragon than the night he was born. Meanwhile, Dragon has grown more powerful."

"Erlan's son is becoming aware of what he is not. Now, it is up to us to find someone who can make him aware of who he is," I told Zophar.

"But the midwife who delivered him and the woman who raised him are both dead. Ormod is the only one in Edenton who knows the young man's identity."

"I have thought long on this subject, Zophar. And my suspicion is this—we must drive the young man from Edenton, at least for a time. We may have no choice. Ormod resents him, and Dragon will not be defeated by the strength of angels."

\* \* \*

Ormod's blacksmith shop rang with the alternating tap of a small hammer on iron and the deep thud of a sledgehammer. On the far side of the anvil, Ormod's son, Alayn, brought the sledge down on the glowing iron with perfect timing. He was a broad youth whose cheeks, nose, and the stubble of hair on his chin were smeared with soot. His father stood facing him. Ormod's stocky frame had grown wider. His beard, now white, reached his chest. The top of his head was bare and shiny. With his left hand he gripped the tongs that held the iron—a brace for the manor house door—on the anvil. With his right hand, he tapped the iron brace with a small hammer to indicate where the sledge should strike next. Neither man spoke, but together they shaped the iron as one.

A fair, light-haired youth watched. His name was Rhys, and though he knew it not, he was the orphaned son of Lord Erlan. He had none of the thick build of the other two men; his muscles were lean and long. Occasionally, he would cough, stoke the fire with a poker and work the bellows.

The blacksmith laid the hammer aside and placed the iron in the fire. He waited for the iron to glow from the heat. A minute passed, but the iron brace failed to glow and the flame flickered and weakened. Ormod scowled at Rhys. "It'll not heat the iron, this fire! Can you do nothing?"

Rhys suddenly came to life and reached for a lump of charcoal to throw on the fire. But Ormod pushed him away and snatched up the black lump. "More charcoal! Move! The iron is cooling."

Rhys stumbled out of the blacksmith shop. Alayn lay down

the hammer and followed. "Rhys!" he hissed when he exited the shop. Rhys did not reply; he turned away from the shop, his shoulders heaving as he breathed deeply.

"Be you deaf? Keep the fire hot! How many times must we tell you?"

Rhys did not look at him. He wiped his eyes with the sleeve of his wool tunic and picked up a chunk of coal.

Alayn pushed Rhys from behind. "Lost your tongue too, 'ave you?"

The shove caused Rhys to lose his balance and stumble. He turned, his eyes red from the smoke, and glared at Alayn. "Why be it always my fault? The fire too cool, the bread too dry, the porridge too thin. Be it my fault he drinks all the time? Be it my fault Mother died?"

Alayn sighed. "I know Father drinks too much. But you'll not need to cry about it."

"Hurry up and get in here!" Ormod shouted from the shop.

"I'm not crying!" Rhys protested.

Alayn picked up two chunks of coal as big as a man's head. "Just make sure you keep the fire hot. I'll be asking him if we can go to the contest at the May Day festival. If you make him mad, he'll not let either of us go!"

Ormod glared at the two young men as they carried the coal into the shop. Rhys fed several lumps of coal to the fire and worked the bellows bringing the flames to life. They watched as the iron began to glow with the heat. Then Ormod lifted the iron brace with his tongs and laid it across the anvil. Alayn lifted the sledge and waited for the sign. With the small hammer, Ormod tapped the iron. Alayn brought the sledge down on the spot.

They worked the iron till it had the shape that Ormod had imagined in his head. Sweat rolled down their faces leaving streaks in the black soot. Finally, Ormod lifted the iron from the anvil and dipped it into a pot of water. The iron hissed and the water steamed.

"Festival ends tomorrow," Alayn said. "There'll be a contest at the end of the festival—a contest between two of Acwellen's prisoners."

Ormod pulled the iron from the water and inspected it. "And what 'ave you heard of this contest?"

"It'll be a contest between two prisoners. The challenger gets to choose the weapon," Alayn replied. "They may use weapons we made here in the shop."

Ormod laid the tongs down with a sigh and looked at Alayn. "Do you know what we make swords and battle axes for, Alayn? Raiders from the north, thieves on the roads between the villages—how will the lords protect their people?" He held the iron in front of him. "That is why we make those weapons." He lowered the iron into the water again. "Not for the entertainment of lords who want to watch men kill each other!" He slammed the tongs on a wooden bench and started for the door.

Alayn followed him. "But the whole village will be there."

Ormod stopped at the door. Alayn and Rhys waited. After several deep breaths, Ormod said quietly, "If that be what you want, then go."

"And Rhys?" Alayn asked, glancing at the fair-haired youth. Rhys shook his head, not wanting Alayn to anger Ormod further—yet hoping Ormod would agree.

Ormod waved them away.

In years past on the final afternoon of the May Day festival, the merchants would take down their tables loaded with leather goods, fabrics, potions, and wines, and people would leave for the nearby villages of Wessex. But this year the crowds stayed. The merchants continued to sell their goods till the afternoon when groups of people began to drift toward the manor house lawn where the contest would take place.

Alayn and Rhys wandered through the merchants' tables. Rhys stopped at a table where a merchant sold medicines in colored bottles. Rhys marveled at the deep green color of a bottle of liquid.

"Ah, take some of that home to your mother, son. It'll cure the child's cough or the old person's ache, and will even put hair on the chest of a young man like you!"

Alayn pulled on Rhys' shoulder. "Come on, fore we miss the contest."

They turned toward the manor house just as several people swerved from the road and jostled them. Five young men were coming, striding abreast along the manor road. Rhys immediately recognized Crosnan, Lord Acwellen's son. Villagers scattered from the path of the parading young men with swords at their sides, shining chain-mail shirts, and green capes flapping in the breeze.

Crosnan had visited the blacksmith's shop a number of times. He had been there to buy swords or have them sharpened. Alayn detested Crosnan's strutting around the shop in his fine clothes. The last time Crosnan had come, Alayn had laid a soot-covered hammer on Crosnan's red woolen cape. When Crosnan noticed it, he was enraged. He picked the hammer up and threw it across the shop. Rhys suspected Alayn had soiled the red cape on purpose. But when he asked Alayn, he only got a smile. Now, as the young men passed, Crosnan's eyes met Alayn's, and he stopped. His friends, and the attention of the crowd, followed Crosnan as he approached Alayn.

"Smith," Crosnan addressed Alayn while unsheathing his sword. "I think my sword needs sharpened."

With that, Crosnan drew his sword and held it up close to Alayn's face. "Steady, Alayn," Rhys whispered. Alayn didn't blink, his face set as stone.

Crosnan lowered his voice, "Know how to use one of these, do you? Or do you just make them?"

Alayn made no reply; both men waited for the other one to move. The crowd watched silently. Zophar and I gripped our sword hilts. Half a dozen devils faced us from behind Crosnan. Suddenly, Crosnan grinned, lowered his sword, feigned a bow toward Alayn, and backed away as he slid the sword back into its sheath. Lord Acwellen's son and his friends fell back into their march toward the manor house.

The crowd slowly came back to life. Alayn, his eyes narrow

and his face flushed, glared after Crosnan. Rhys watched Alayn but said nothing.

"We'd better go, lest we be late for the contest," Alayn said bitterly.

They walked to the manor house lawn where crowds of people gathered. Stakes had been driven into the ground, forming a large circle; ropes were tied from one stake to the next to form a sort of fence. On the far side of the roped area, there was a wooden platform upon which sat Lord Acwellen, Lady Gwendolyn, Crosnan, and the shire reeve.

The reeve, a tall, heavy man who seemed to take up most of the stage, stood and raised his hands. The crowd hushed.

"Friends," the reeve began. Rhys thought his high-pitched voice seemed odd for such a large man. "As the finale of the May Day festival, we bring you a battle worthy of this great event. Derian the stable hand has challenged Earm, the lord's debtor, to a duel with the mace."

A murmur of surprise went through the crowd. Alayn glanced at Rhys and shrugged. Of all the rumored contestants, Derian was not one of them. No one in the crowd had heard that Acwellen's muscular young stable hand had been in the manor keep. The man he had challenged was a skinny, awkward man—the town drunk. No one had ever seen Earm lift a mace, let alone use one. His drunkenness had led to his debt to Acwellen. Only a month ago, Acwellen had him thrown into the keep.

Acwellen, Gwendolyn, and those on the stage applauded. Green and red banners, Acwellen's standards, flapped in the wind. The reeve turned to the right side of the stage and motioned. One of Acwellen's thanes, dressed in a green and red tunic under a chain mail shirt, stepped forward with the confident-looking Derian. The stable hand carried the mace over his shoulder. It occurred to Rhys that Derian preferred this contest to pitching manure from Acwellen's stables. The reeve turned and motioned to the left side of the stage. Another thane stepped forward; this one much more slowly. He was leading Earm toward the arena by a rope tied to

Earm's wrists. Earm shuffled slowly at the end of the rope. He was pale, and his wide eyes stared at the scene around him.

"He looks of terror," Rhys whispered to Alayn.

Alayn nodded, "He looks sober."

Another thane carrying the mace walked behind Earm. The thanes and prisoners met in the middle of the arena. Earm cowered behind one of the thanes.

"This contest shall be to the finish!" the reeve cried. Everyone knew what he meant. "Let the contest begin!"

Rhys glanced around the manor lawn at the men, women, and children watching, and he felt sick. They were neighbors, kinsmen, and friends. They had grown up together and their parents had grown up together. They knew Derian and Earm's families. And now, for the sake of sport, Acwellen pitted the two against each other as if they were no more than a pair of fighting cocks. *It could be anyone,* he realized, *even Alayn and me. And we watch as if it be a dance or juggling act by a traveling jester.*

Rhys leaned over to Alayn and whispered, "I'll be leaving."

The thane next to Earm dropped the mace at Earm's feet and stepped back. Derian began to swing the mace through the air. Earm stared at Derian like a hare cornered by a hound. He dropped to his knees and fumbled with the handle of the mace. Derian approached, now swinging the mace round and round over his head. Earm started up, straining to lift the mace. Derian leaped at Earm swinging the mace for his head. Earm stumbled and fell. Derian's mace slipped from his hand and hurtled across the arena.

"Ouuuww!" howled a man in the crowd as the mace landed on his foot.

Alayn turned and frowned at Rhys for interrupting. "What?" he asked, impatiently.

"I don't want to see this. I'll be leaving."

Derian ran across the arena to retrieve the mace. Earm got to his feet. He looked wildly around and then started running in the opposite direction of Derian. Two thanes ran after him as he attempted to slide under the rope.

Rhys wondered for an instant if he could pull Earm under

the ropes, and they could run fast enough to escape the thanes. But the thanes were there too quick, pulling Earm back into the arena. Derian came charging toward them swinging the mace over his head. The thanes quickly let go of Earm and got out of the way. One of them fell behind Earm. Earm stood suddenly and turned toward Derian just as Derian released the mace. It slammed into Earm's chest knocking him back over the thane and firmly to the ground. He lay motionless.

Derian stopped. The crowd was silent. The thane stood and looked down at the fallen debtor. Then the sound of clapping came from the stage. Crosnan was standing. "Bravo! Bravo!" he shouted. Acwellen stood and began clapping. Then everyone on the stage stood and began cheering the stable hand.

Rhys felt a knot in his stomach. He wondered if Earm's mother, when she gave birth to her son, looked at the infant and imagined such an ending for him.

Alayn glared at Rhys. "If you want to leave, then go!"

Rhys looked at Alayn in a way that made them both feel guilty, for they each knew now what Ormod had meant. This was killing simply for the entertainment of a lord. It made Alayn angry. He pushed Rhys away from him and said, "Go on!"

# Chapter 3

## THE HUNT

I thought long on how to make Rhys aware of whose son he was. In the end, I realized there was little I could do; I needed help from other angels or even from my Captain. But I could give him something that would connect him to his father's world. For this, I chose the weapon used by lords and noblemen—a bow.

Shooting arrows with a bow required more skill than most villagers of Edenton had. Other than Acwellen and his household, the men of Edenton used spears to hunt, just as their fathers had. Every man knew how to use a spear if he could get close enough to his prey. With the tension created by the bending of the bow, a hunter did not have to get as close. The arrow could be sent farther and with more accuracy than the spear. But it required practice, and it required a bow, which Rhys did not have until the day a nobleman, at least that is what he appeared to be to the people of Edenton, visited Ormod's shop. He brought a shield to be straightened. While the nobleman waited, he showed Rhys his bow and instructed him on how to use it. "Archery requires a keen eye and a steady hand," the nobleman had said. And so it seems that Rhys was born with both. This nobleman was so impressed that he gave Rhys his bow and a dozen iron-tipped arrows.

Ormod had no use for the bow or the "ways of noblemen," but he was quite fond of venison and was pleased that Rhys had begun using the bow to bring venison to their table. Alayn tried the bow as well. And being bigger and stronger than Rhys, he could send an arrow farther, but he could not hold the bow steady enough to hit a target. Alayn's lack of skill caused Rhys to work all the harder at this one thing he knew he could do better. Rhys practiced until he could put an arrow to the string and release it in one swift motion.

Several weeks after May Day, Ormod decided to send Rhys and Alayn hunting. Zophar went into the forest ahead of them to see if any wolves or bear were lurking there.

"Behold Rhys the archer!" Alayn announced, bowing in mock reverence as they crossed the meadow to the forest.

Rhys ignored Alayn. He was happy because they were going hunting, and even Alayn's taunting couldn't lessen his love for hunting. It seemed to him the only thing he did well.

"Rhys," Alayn grinned, "rhymes with 'lies.'"

He pointed at Rhys' bow. "You have twelve arrows and a bow. I have one spear. You can hunt for twelve little rabbits, and I'll hunt for one large stag!"

When they reached the forest, Alayn led the way to the stream they had visited often. They knew that deer came here to drink. They also knew that the soft banks of the stream would cause the deer to leave tracks.

\* \* \*

Through the dark forest I saw Zophar with his fiery red hair walking quickly but quietly toward me. He pointed back the way he had come. "The reeve and his thanes are ahead—fifteen riders with sword and spear. Acwellen sent them here to catch poachers of his deer."

"But this is freeman's land...." I stopped and looked at Rhys and Alayn. They were walking into a trap, I realized.

I asked which way the men were headed. Zophar pointed in the other direction. Were there devils about? I asked. He had counted more than a dozen. He said that he would follow the reeve's men if I would guard Rhys and Alayn. I agreed, and he disappeared into the forest.

\* \* \*

A moment later Alayn crossed the brook and searched along the far bank for deer tracks. "Remember playing Beowulf here?" he asked.

"Aye. I had to stand in the water and be the monster Grendel."

"You asked to be Grendel," Alayn lied. Suddenly he stopped and pointed down, "Tracks." Rhys crossed the stream and looked where Alayn was pointing. He saw both deer and wolf tracks. Alayn started up the bank of the stream. He stopped when he reached a broad path that led through the forest. "The path is too hard and dry; there be no tracks here."

Rhys followed him to the path. "Which way do you think they went?"

"Who knows? They could have followed the path and then turned into the forest at any time."

Rhys looked across the path at a thicket of undergrowth. "Maybe they went into this thicket."

"Do you see any tracks?"

"No."

Alayn looked at Rhys. "Then what makes you think they went into the thicket here?"

"I don't know," Rhys replied, gazing into the dark brush. "But I think that is the way the deer went. Perhaps we should split up. I could go into the thicket and look for the deer. You take the path and look for tracks."

Alayn shook his head. "Your bow won't be any good in that brush. Take the path where you can make use of your arrows, and I'll wander through this brush. If anything be in there, I'll flush it out to you in the open."

Rhys turned again and gazed into the dark undergrowth. "The wolf could be in there," he said. "Maybe we should both follow the path until we see some sign of the deer."

Alayn glared at him. "You're worse than an old woman! A moment ago you said you thought the deer went into the thicket. Now you think we should both follow the path? Do you see any signs of deer on the path?"

"Nay," Rhys replied, frowning.

"Then I'll go into the thicket. Be ready with your bow."

"Aye, I'll follow the path," Rhys conceded. "But watch yourself in there."

"If the deer is too big for that bow, give a whistle and I'll come out and kill it with this," Alayn said, holding up the spear and grinning.

Rhys did not reply. He turned and started down the path that the reeve had taken moments before. Alayn raised his spear and started into the brush.

\* \* \*

I watched Alayn go, knowing I would have to stay with Rhys. But I could follow Alayn's movement through the brush by his sound. I knew he did not have the patience to move quietly.

"Iothiel!"

I looked up the path and saw Zophar running toward me. "The reeve and his men have spread out and are headed back this way!" he shouted.

Suddenly I heard a devil scream and turned to see a winged shadow coming at me from behind. The devil slashed at my head with a sword. I blocked the devil's sword with my own.

"Save Rhys!" I shouted at Zophar.

But before he could act, a second devil rushed upon us. Zophar clashed swords with it. My own attacker fell back with the first blow from my sword. I brought another one down upon the devil before it could set itself. It stumbled, and I ended the fight with my next strike.

I turned to see Zophar besting the other devil. Meanwhile, Rhys was walking unknowingly into the path of the reeve and his thanes. I had only a few seconds to get him off the path.

* * *

Rhys noticed a shape in the path and bent down to inspect it. It was too big for a deer track, he thought to himself. It looked more like a horse hoof. At that moment, as he told it later, he had an odd feeling that he was being watched. He lifted his head slowly. There, not more than twenty yards ahead of him, stood the largest stag he had ever seen. The great stag looked straight into Rhys' eyes and took a step toward him. Rhys stared, his heart beating wildly. He slowly slid an arrow from his quiver, placed it on the bowstring, and lifted his bow to take aim. He hesitated. The stag continued to look at him. The animal seemed to be waiting on him. His hands shook slightly as he released the arrow—it struck harmlessly in the ground in front of the stag. The stag took a step back, then turned to the forest along the stream and disappeared with two great leaps. Rhys retrieved the arrow and ran to the place where the stag entered the wood. He could see the stag walking among beech trees forty feet ahead of him.

Rhys slipped quietly through the trees, hoping to get close enough to the stag to get another shot. The animal did not run but kept a deliberate pace away from the path. Rhys thought of the praise and reputation he would get if he were to kill such a great stag. He was already known as a skilled archer. But with this kill, he would be known throughout Wessex as a great hunter.

Rhys had gone about one hundred yards from the path when he heard Alayn cry out. The cry sounded of desperation—that was not like Alayn. Rhys waited and listened, keeping an eye on the spot where he had last seen the stag. *What if Alayn is trying to trick me?* he wondered. But he heard other voices, the voices of men shouting.

Rhys took a couple of steps backward, still watching for the stag. But he felt sure Alayn really was in need, so he whirled about and ran back toward the path. As he did, a large tree limb caught him in the forehead. He pitched backward to the ground, and darkness settled over his mind.

\* \* \*

I stood above unconscious Rhys, my sword in hand. The danger that he might happen into the thanes was past, at least for now. I heard no longer the sound of swords clashing. Zophar approached slowly. He was dim; his energy drained from the fight. Behind him, two angels stood guard with their swords raised.

Zophar looked down at Rhys. "Is he alright?" he asked in a low voice.

I nodded. "I had to keep him from going back. How many devils were there?"

Zophar slumped against a tree. "About a dozen. Gabriel sent angels from Edenton and Iconium to help. The devils that are left are guarding the reeve and his thanes. The reeve captured Alayn. One of the thanes said he saw someone else, another hunter, so some of his men are still out looking."

"I'll guard Rhys. You're too weak to fight now. Go to Orion and be restored. One of the angels from Edenton can take you."

"A guardian from Iconium is watching over Alayn," Zophar said slowly. "There is nothing more we can do for him. But Rhys…."

"I'll watch over him. Go!"

\* \* \*

Voices slowly made their way into Rhys' mind. He opened his eyes, but saw only shapes in the darkness. He remembered that he and Alayn had been hunting deer. He remembered seeing the stag and then hearing Alayn cry out. He remembered hearing shouting; then there was the tree limb. Now, with his head throbbing, he realized the voices were coming nearer to him.

"See anything over there?" a voice asked.

"Nay! Not in this wretched darkness."

Rhys lay still listening to muffled sounds and cursing.

The second voice spoke again. "We got one. What do they need any more for? Acwellen can hang the one we got. One prisoner makes as good an example as two, if you ask me."

"Ask you?' scolded the first voice. "Your woman doesn't even ask you when to plant leeks. Told me that yourself. You think Acwellen or the reeve'll be asking your opinion? We'll keep looking till we find the other one or the reeve tells us to stop."

The first voice cursed back, "The reeve can look for him his self! It's too dark for me. Back to the fire I'll go."

The men struggled through the dark past Rhys. He heard twigs snapping, an occasional thump, and then "ouch!" as one of the men ran into a tree.

When their sounds faded, Rhys sat up slowly and touched the bump on his forehead. The pain went from the front of his head to the back and down his neck. He leaned back against a tree and stared into the darkness. The eerie hooting of an owl came from the trees above him.

He said to himself, "We weren't poaching. This be freeman's land." He wiped his cheeks and sniffled for so long I began to grow impatient. He was too close to the path to still be sitting here in the morning.

I bent close to him and whispered, "They will begin looking again in the morning. Your best chance is to get away while it's still dark."

I don't know if he heard my voice, but he felt the ground for his bow and arrows. "Mother Mary!" he swore. His bow was broken in two. Rhys realized that he had fallen on it. He picked up the quiver and the arrows scattered on the ground. To his left he could see the faint light from a campfire. That meant he was facing the way back to the stream and Edenton. He wondered about Alayn; shouldn't he do something to help him? But he heard no answer, so he began walking as quietly as he could through the dark toward the stream.

# Chapter 4

## THE PARTING

The moon hid behind iron-gray clouds when we reached the meadow outside of Edenton. I looked about for signs of the enemy. We had managed, for the moment, to escape the trap the devils had set for Rhys in the forest. But with the dragon in Edenton, things could change quickly. Rhys crossed the dark meadow as quietly as he could so he wouldn't wake the village dogs. When he reached the cottage, he pulled at the latch on the door, but the bolt was closed. He peered through a crack and saw a flickering candle on the table. He hissed into the crack, "Sir! Unbolt the door! Let me in!"

Rhys heard a familiar rasping sound—Ormod snoring. He rattled the latch and cried. "Sir! 'Tis Rhys! Please let me in!"

The snoring stopped. The candle flickered and almost went out. Rhys could hear a chair fall over and Ormod shuffling toward the door. There was the sound of the bolt sliding open. The latch came up, and the door opened.

Ormod's face was dark as he stood with the glow of the candlelight behind him.

"Eh…who's there?" he growled into the night.

"Rhys."

"Where 'ave you been?"

The stale smell of ale washed over Rhys. He realized how

tired and thirsty he was.

"Deer hunting."

"Middle a' the night…." Ormod mumbled, rubbing his face with his hands. "Where be my son?"

The last question confused Rhys, but he replied, "Here, sir."

"You? You be Erlan's son. Where be Alayn?"

Rhys stared at the old man. He tried to clear his mind and think, but he couldn't stop wondering what Ormod meant by "You be Erlan's son."

"Well…where be my son?!"

Rhys swallowed, "Alayn?"

"Aye! Alayn, my son!" Ormod repeated impatiently. "Where be Alayn?"

"They have him," Rhys said quietly.

"They? They who? Who 'as Alayn?"

"The reeve and the lord's thanes."

Rhys could see Ormod focus and come fully awake; his labored breathing paused. "What happened?" Ormod asked with an air of fear mixed with anger.

Rhys swallowed again and drew a deep breath. "I didn't see them. Alayn and I split up. I chased a…."

He hesitated. Sometimes when Rhys felt himself trapped, like a fox pursued by hounds, he would blurt out something he knew was not true. Perhaps he believed that he did not quite measure up to the world around him; and so he would say something that made him seem a little more important. He tried to stop himself, but the words just came out, "I chased a…a *white*…stag…like the one Rynelf saw! It was the biggest, whitest stag anyone's ever seen…then I heard Alayn yell…."

Ormod's beard rose as he tightened his lips. Rhys felt like a fool for calling it a white stag—he realized that Ormod was not one to believe such stories. There was a desperate tightening in Rhys' chest, but he went on.

"I hit my head. And then I heard two thanes talking. They said the reeve was looking for poachers. But we weren't poaching; we were just beyond the stream—where we always hunt. They said Acwellen wants to claim the land for his own...."

Ormod glared at Rhys. The candle flickered. "You expect me to believe stories about a white stag, do you lad?"

"But the reeve...."

"You see the reeve?"

"Nay. But I hit my head and heard voices...."

"Heard voices? Saw a white stag? Do you think I be daft?"

"But I did hear voices."

The back of Ormod's right hand hit Rhys' jaw and spun him around. He found himself on the ground on his hands and knees. The door to the cottage slammed shut. Rhys could hear the bolt sliding closed. The house was silent. Ormod had locked him out.

Rhys got up and waited by the door like a whipped dog waiting for its master.

"Father? Please let me in. Father!" Rhys' cries met only cold, dark silence.

He was alone. He sank to his knees and bowed his head to the ground. His shoulders began to shake as a sob rose in his throat. Another sob came and then another until his whole body shook. He wept deeply. He wept till his tears were gone and he felt nothing but emptiness.

Rhys stood and wandered through the village. I followed him past darkened cottages. A dog barked once before running up to Rhys and sniffing at him. It wagged its tail and followed him past the last of the cottages. Rhys reached the road to Iconium. I hoped that he would start for Iconium—hoped that his tears would be enough to drive him away from Edenton; perhaps drive him to someone who could form him into the man who would face Dragon. But Rhys stumbled onto a path that led to a hiding place where he and Alayn used to play. He crawled through a thicket and into a clearing where stood three trees. He leaned against a tree and gazed into the darkness. He wondered if the prayers his mother taught him would help him now.

* * *

I had watched Rhys when the midwife handed him to Ormod seventeen years ago. I had grown fond of the boy with his great imagination. He loved stories of adventure—of good lords and their thanes fighting against the raiders from the north; of Beowulf fighting the evil Grendel. He played for hours making up stories and acting them out. So it was hard for me to watch the pain he had to go through to make him into a man capable of facing Dragon. It is always difficult for angels to watch over humans in deep sorrow. And though Ormod had raised the boy and kept him safe, he was impatient with the boy's daydreams. The man's efforts to drive the boy's thoughts toward smithing left them both frustrated, till this night when Ormod's anger exploded in a drunken rage.

* * *

The clouds passed and the moon, like a candle, cast its light down on the tree where the young man lay. No flutter of bat or movement of tree limb escaped my notice. I watched Rhys sleep as one whose fitful spirit will not let him fully rest.

Rhys woke at dawn with hunger gnawing at him. He stretched, felt the knot on his forehead recalling yesterday's events, and knew he was not dreaming. He found a nearby stream and drank his fill. The water cooled Rhys' throat, but made his empty stomach feel water logged. He crawled back through the thicket to the road that went to Iconium. The road was deserted so he rose and stood behind a large tree.

I do not know what he thought at that moment. He was one who wanted to believe in the good of things. After all, he had forgiven Alayn's many mockings and bruises. Maybe it was his nature that caused him to go back. Maybe it was his hunger. Whatever it was, it caught me so by surprise that I nearly panicked. Rhys stepped out into the road and began walking back toward Edenton. I drew my sword and hoped the Spirit would speak to him in an audible voice if necessary. He passed a cottage. The dog that followed him last night ran past with a small, dirty boy running after it.

Suddenly Rhys stopped. In front of his cottage, he saw four horses. A thane, dressed in a green and red tunic and chain-mail shirt, held the horses' reins. The thane looked up, and his eyes met Rhys'. For a brief moment they stared at one another. Rhys took a step back. The thane motioned toward him and yelled, "You there! Come here!"

Rhys turned and ran back toward the road to Iconium. I saw several devils standing among the cottages, watching curiously. I backed away, sword in hand, hoping their curiosity would not lead to an attack.

Rhys ran wildly up the road. Just as he veered off the road and into the forest, he heard men yelling behind him and the sound of horses' hooves.

He slowed only to dodge thickets and duck under trees. He splashed into a stream and waded along it as fast as he could. It would be hard for the thanes to find his tracks in the stream. He fell, rose soaking wet and tried to run upstream again. A dozen yards later he splashed out of the stream on the other side of the bank. He heard a distant cry. Away from the stream, away from the road and the thanes, he ran. Thorns clawed at him. A branch whipped his face. There was a rock, but he saw it too late. He stepped on it, his left ankle twisted, and he fell.

Rhys rolled on the ground, groaning and clutching his ankle. He crawled behind a thicket, panting, watching the wood behind him, and listening. The only thing he heard was a bird crowing. There were no voices, no sound of thanes looking for him. He reached down and touched the ankle. It was beginning to swell. He lay back on the ground and stared into the limbs of a tree.

"Fool. Fool!" he said to himself. "Can't go back, ever. I be a cursed fool."

There was a cool shift in the wind. A drop of rain wetted his arm. His stomach growled. Rhys sat up, which lessened his hunger pangs. He held his ankle and rocked back and forth to comfort himself. More raindrops fell till a slow, steady rain spread across the forest, washing it clean.

\* \* \*

Amidst the patter of the rain, I heard a rumbling laugh. I turned and saw red-haired Zophar coming through the forest. His eyes shone with the light of joy. I knew immediately that he had been in the Presence, the very throne of heaven. He had seen the one who is much greater than even the archangels Michael and Gabriel. Zophar had been in the presence of the Creator. I too have been in the Presence, and I knew there was no use asking Zophar about it; it was beyond words. *How do you describe something that wounds you in a way that heals?* I wondered. *A blinding light that causes you to see what you have never seen before?*

"Not so long ago, Zophar, you said we guardians should not amuse ourselves with light-hearted revelry," I reminded him, "but ever be vigilant."

He smiled at me all the more. Then his shoulders started shaking. Waves of laughter rolled up inside him and tumbled out. It made me smile despite Rhys' troubles.

I tried again, "Our circumstance is difficult here, you know. Rhys has eaten nothing for a day and a half, his ankle is twisted, the reeve's thanes are hunting him; and one has seen his face. He faces grave danger, Zophar."

Zophar nodded, unable to speak. Tears flowed down his cheeks.

I found it starting to rise up in me as well. "You don't seem...concerned," I stuttered, trying myself to keep from laughing.

He shook his head, took a breath, and said, "It is fortunate...that Rhys...knows how to run." He took another breath. "Gabriel gave me the name of one who may help. Shall I find him?"

The hilarious light of the Spirit washed over me. The weight of the mission, the pain of facing hideous demons, the burden of guarding the hunted Rhys—all of it lifted. I sighed peacefully and said, "Meet us on the road to Iconium."

# Chapter 5

## THE CAVE

My heart was lightened by the heavenly joy, but the same was not true for poor Rhys. While the rain lessened to a steady mist, he sat slumped over trying to keep his face dry. Though his life had never been easy, he had rarely gone hungry and had always had a cottage for shelter. But now, even those comforts were gone. It was what men call *luck*; "bad luck" when life is difficult and "good luck" when one is at ease in life. In truth, all times, both good and bad, are in the Creator's hands.

This present trial made me all the more anxious to get Rhys started to Iconium. Where else could he go? He couldn't stay in the forest, for he had no food. And he couldn't go back to Edenton. But he just sat there, staring at the ground and wiping the mist and tears from his face. Maybe he had simply given up. Whatever the case, I knew I had to get him started to Iconium soon.

* * *

Rhys felt his swollen ankle again. It throbbed with the steady beating of his heart. He leaned his back against the tree and stared at the ground, trying to think of something other than pain. But a feeling crept over him that he was not alone, that he was being watched. Rhys lifted his head slowly. His heart stopped as he gazed into the dark, glassy eyes of a large wolf. The wolf studied him from a distance of twenty feet. Its gray head was lowered, and Rhys could see the powerful shoulders just above eye level. He wondered if it knew he was injured.

"Aaahhh!" Rhys shouted at the animal. He pushed himself up on his good leg while holding onto the tree. He looked around for a rock to throw, but saw none. He reached into the quiver lying on the ground and pulled out an arrow. Holding the arrow like a spear, he flung it desperately at the wolf. "Get away! Go!" The arrow landed harmlessly between Rhys and the wolf. The wolf backed up a few paces, hesitated, and then disappeared into the forest.

"I'll not die," he declared. "Not here at least."

He glanced around and saw a broken tree limb that was about five feet long. He hobbled over and picked it up. Taking his knife from his belt, he sharpened one end of the limb to make a crude spear. Supporting himself with the spear's sharp side up, Rhys found that he could walk if he went slowly. He retrieved the arrow and counted eight more in the quiver. The other three had fallen out when he hit his head on the tree limb.

Rhys limped northward in the direction of Iconium. He had never been to Iconium, but he had heard there was an abbey near it. Maybe he could beg some food there. He knew he had to get away from Edenton, and he had to stay off the road where the reeve and his thanes would likely be searching for him.

The trees provided some shelter from the rain. Occasionally Rhys came to growths of tangled, thick brush that he had to limp around. Even though the thickets slowed his progress, he was glad for them. They would provide a place to hide quickly if he saw a thane. The mist ended, and Rhys tried not to think about food or the pain in his ankle. He thought of Ormod, Alayn, and the events of the past day till his mind grew numb.

He had never been beyond Edenton. He wondered how far

he would have to go to escape Edenton's reeve—a town? Two towns? To the very sea? What if he joined an abbey and became a monk? Would he be safe then? Would he be allowed to join an abbey for protection or would it have to be from faith? Rhys glanced up at the sky and saw a hawk staring back at him from the top of a tree. *I be no better than a mouse*, he told himself, *depending on the cover of the forest and my own luck for survival.*

A few hours later, Rhys came to a small stream and drank from it before looking around. The sky was so heavily clouded that Rhys could only guess how soon the sun would set. Across the stream was a steep bank a dozen feet high with a wooded hill at the top. Rhys looked downstream and saw that the water ran toward the road. He looked upstream. There the stream curved back away from him. Although the bank on the opposite side of the stream was steep, going upstream would take him further away from the road. Going downstream would keep him near the road, but he might be seen.

Rhys winced as he placed weight on his swollen left ankle. He drew a deep breath before beginning to limp upstream, away from the road to Iconium. Heavy drops of rain fell as he rounded the bend in the stream and came into a clearing. In a moment, Rhys' tunic was soaked till it clung to him. Water streaked down his face from his matted hair.

He leaned against a tree and stared blankly at the rain drops hitting the surface of the stream. The rain grew heavier and louder till he thought he would go deaf. He watched water pool on the opposite bank and overflow into the stream. He closed his eyes to rest, but the image of the wolf sprang into his mind, and he felt wolves creeping toward him through the forest. Rhys opened his eyes and searched the forest around him. There were no wolves, but he became aware of a black hole in the embankment across the stream. It looked like a shadow from a large rock sticking out of the ground. Rhys decided to see if the rock would provide shelter. As soon as the rain lessened, Rhys waded carefully across the stream.

The overhang was nearly hidden from view by two pine trees. A pile of ashes in front of the rock indicated others had built a fire while camping there. Rhys found the hole to be a hollowed out area like a den and just large enough for a person to huddle under to keep dry. Rhys peered into the blackness until his eyes began to adjust. Then he realized it was an opening to a cave.

Rhys did not like dark, closed spaces. So he sat under the overhanging rock and watched the rain fall. But water, seeping in behind the rock, began to drip on his face. He knew the cave, though dark, would be dry and would put him out of sight of wolves or thanes. If he slept under the overhanging rock, he was in full view of anyone passing by. He moved a little, and for a moment he seemed to have escaped the dripping water. But, just as he became comfortable enough to begin nodding off, a cold drop of water hit his neck and slid down his back. His head snapped up. He turned and crawled fifteen feet into the cave till it curved into a second chamber. Rhys felt his way around the bend, curled up on the dry floor, and fell asleep.

In a dream, Rhys saw Alayn hanging on the edge of a cliff. Alayn cried out for help, but Rhys, though he tried his best, could not reach him. Alayn began to slip when Rhys heard a cry from above. He looked up and saw a dragon flying toward him across a dark sky. It had the face of a man, but fire came from its mouth. It swooped down, plucking Alayn from the cliff in its talons. As it flew away with Alayn, Rhys ran into the forest after them. A great sound came from the sky. Rhys stopped and looked up. The sound was the flapping of the dragon's wings as it flew just above the treetops. Rhys turned to run but stumbled and fell. Above him the dragon slowly flapped its great black wings and breathed fire down at him.

Suddenly, Rhys was wide-awake, his heart pounding. *All a dream...just a dream*, he told himself. For a few seconds, he struggled to remember where he was. It must be night; the cave was dark. Then something took his breath and made his heart stop—he heard a shuffling, scraping sound coming from the mouth of the cave. Something was entering the cave, dragging itself into the dark chamber. He pulled his hunting knife from his belt and clutched it tightly to keep it from slipping from his sweaty palm. Rhys' every muscle was taut. The image of the dragon staring down at him would not leave his head. He held his breath waiting for the moment he could leap on the thing and try to drive his knife into its heart. He saw its outline, hesitated, and then let out a slight breath. He recognized the shadowy shape of a man. The man bent over a bundle he dragged behind him. Rhys guessed the man was arranging a blanket on the floor. He saw the man unbuckle a belt from his waist and lower a sword to the floor. Rhys stared at the spot where the man had laid the sword. Common villagers did not carry swords. *This must be a lord's thane*, he thought, *or it may be a thief or murderer, someone who prefers to not be seen by the reeve.* Even though he tried to hold his breath quietly within him, he could feel his heart beating loudly in his chest.

The man settled on the floor and lay still. Within a minute a slow, steady snore came from him. Rhys quietly leaned against the rock and slid his knife back into his belt. He looked at where the sword lay on the cave floor. *If only I had that sword*, he thought, *I could defend myself or perhaps sneak up on a hare and kill it. When I got to Iconium, I could sell it and buy food.*

A voice inside Rhys told him that it would be wrong to take the sword. The sword did not belong to him; taking it would be theft. He quickly reminded himself that he was desperate, and the man who had it may well intend to do harm with it. Rhys had nothing to get food or money with, except the hunting knife, a few arrows, and a sharpened stick. *That sword*, he thought, *may be my only hope.*

Rhys took a careful step toward the man. With another step, he stood next to the man. He winced from the pain in the ankle. The man continued snoring. Rhys carefully raised and lowered his right foot over the man. He shifted his weight to his right foot, so he could lift his left foot over him. Rhys watched the regular rise and fall of the man's side as the breath rattled through his throat. Rhys exhaled quietly in relief and reached for the sword.

Suddenly a grip as powerful as any smith's had his right ankle, jerking it violently backwards and causing Rhys to scream in pain. *Now I am going to die*, he thought as he fell forward. He tried to push himself up, but the man was on top of him, holding him down. Rhys felt the sharp, cold edge of a knife at his throat.

"Relieve me of the burden of me sword, eh? Know what the punishment be for thieving? Parting your hand from your arm. You'll not likely steal with that hand again, I reckon."

Rhys swallowed hard. The stranger's threat made a cold knot form in his stomach.

"Have you nothing to say for yourself?"

Rhys swallowed again and whispered, "If you be one of Lord Acwellen's thanes, I swear to you that Alayn and I weren't poaching. We weren't on the lord's land. Nor did we break any of the lord's laws."

"Acwellen?"

Something in the stranger's deep, coarse voice gave Rhys hope. "Aye," he said as loudly as he could with a knife at his throat.

The stranger hesitated, then lowered the knife and sat back. Rhys sat up and rubbed his neck. The stranger moved the sword out of Rhys' reach and sat looking at him. In the faint light of the cave, the man appeared to be about Ormod's age. But Rhys thought he looked taller.

"Tell me about this poaching, or not poaching, on Acwellen's land," he commanded. "And tell me what it has to do with stealing my sword."

Rhys wiped a shaking hand across his forehead. He took a deep breath and waited for the lightness in his head to pass. He wondered what he said to cause the stranger's sudden change in behavior towards him—he didn't want to say anything that would undo the change.

"My brother, Alayn, and I went on a hunt in the freeman's forest near Edenton. He went into the brush to flush out the deer." Rhys paused, thinking of Ormod's reaction to his story of the stag and his comment about not being Rhys' father. *Tell only what be necessary*, he thought.

He continued, "I saw a deer on the road and followed it into the forest. I heard Alayn yell. I turned to go to him and ran into a tree limb, knocking myself out." Rhys rubbed the small bump still on his forehead. "When I came to, I heard two of the thanes talking. They said that one hunter had been found and that Acwellen could use him to make an example of poachers. But that wasn't Acwellen's land. Men from Edenton have always hunted in that part of the forest. We weren't poaching!"

The stranger nodded. "Wouldn't matter to Acwellen. That snake! But go on."

"I walked back to our cottage. But Ormod was drunk and got angry when I told him about Alayn." Rhys thought again about Ormod saying that he was a lord's son, but he pushed the thought aside and continued, "He told me to get out. I slept out in the forest last night. In the morning, I tried to go back, but Acwellen's thanes were there. One saw me, and I got scared and ran."

Rhys hesitated. The stranger waited, so he went on. "I have no food or money; no weapon for hunting, nowhere to go. I thought…if I had…when I saw your sword, I thought I could get some food…."

The stranger held up his hand in a motion to stop Rhys from talking. Rhys stopped, relieved to not have to say more. The man reached under his blanket and pulled out a pouch. He handed it to Rhys. "The pouch holds some fruit and bread. Do not eat too much or too fast, lest you become sick. I'll be going to the abbey in Iconium, and the brothers would have enough for both of us to eat there. The brothers are an odd lot. But their food'll stay with you."

"But the harvest hasn't come yet. 'Tis the hungry season," Rhys reminded the stranger. "No one has enough food this time of year."

The stranger snorted. "You don't know the brothers. They are very good at living on small portions of food. And they are generous—they will go without before turning a guest away hungry."

Rhys was amazed to hear that anyone had food to share at this time of year. In Edenton, it had been a fact of life that only Lord Acwellen and those in the manor house had enough food in the weeks before the first harvest. But the stranger provided no more explanation. He simply stretched out on the blanket and, moments later, was snoring again.

* * *

I watched Rhys quickly devour some bread and cheese along with some little wrinkled pieces of fruit he had never seen before. He wanted to eat more, much more, but I guessed that he was unwilling to take the last bit of the stranger's food. He lay back on the cave floor, listened to the stranger's snore, and felt his shrunken stomach rumble at the food. He looked at the dark shape where the stranger lay and wondered how the man could sleep so easily only minutes after Rhys had tried to steal his sword.

Stooping down, I stepped from the mouth of the cave and looked through the trees to the clouds and stars above. I wondered where Zophar was, and I wondered if this was the man whom he sought.

# Chapter 6

## TO ICONIUM

That night I wandered along the stream that ran just outside the cave. The sky cleared, and high above the earth hung a round moon, perfectly positioned. I wondered if Zophar, wherever he was, had noticed it; or if he knew the angel who watched over its orbit. The stars were as bright as diamonds. It was the contrast in the night sky that fascinated me; how the Creator could make a sky so black filled with stars that were so brilliant. I saw a shooting star fall from the sky and thought of Zorran. I shuddered as I wondered where he was and what he had become. All those angels who, like Zorran, rebelled and fell from the heavens were like stars swept from the night sky—a third of the diamonds snatched from the dark firmament. What loss; what beauty and strength wasted.

While I paced the stream bank, the moon slid down behind a tree, and the sky turned lighter shades of blue. I glanced about the forest for signs of devils. The stranger's gray horse stood up under the tree it was tied to and shook itself. I worried that Zophar had not returned and wondered if he could have grown weary of this mission. *He's been faithful thus far, but it has only been seventeen years*, I thought.

\* \* \*

Rhys sat up suddenly and looked around. He thought he heard Alayn's voice, but he didn't see Alayn. Then it all came back to him—the long walk from Edenton, the cave, and the stranger. When Rhys realized the stranger had left, he grabbed his spear and hobbled out of the cave.

Across the stream from the cave, the man was saddling a large, gray horse. He had the broad shoulders of one who had spent hours working with a sword. He wore a chain mail shirt over a brown tunic. His sword sheath was fixed to a leather belt. The stranger turned to Rhys, and Rhys saw a scar running over his right cheekbone, just above a beard streaked with gray, and over his right eye where the eyebrow should be. The eyebrow was missing and all that was left was the scar. Rhys stared for a moment before he caught himself.

"Are you a lord's thane?" he asked.

The stranger's hesitation made Rhys think he was trying to recall something from the past. "My name is Bors," he said simply. He turned back to the horse and tightened the girth strap. "The only thanes you know be the ones in Edenton, eh?"

"A man who came to my father's smith shop once told of thanes across the sea who fought on horseback wearing heavy suits of metal. Those suits…we never made anything like that. That be quite a job to smith a suit for a man to wear."

"I've heard the stories," Bors replied. "I don't know how a man could fight in a metal suit. This chain mail be enough for me."

Rhys watched for a moment before asking, "Do you live in Iconium?"

Bors finished with the saddle and turned to Rhys. "I've business at the abbey, though I will only be there a few days." He glanced at the rough-hewn spear Rhys was leaning on.

"I saw a wolf," Rhys explained.

Bors raised his eyebrow. "A wolf, eh? You need a weapon to fend them off when you travel alone this way. I prefer a sword. A spear will do, but I've never seen one used with arrows."

Rhys felt his face flush red as he glanced down at the quiver of arrows. "I broke my bow," he said sheepishly.

"A bow? You learned to use a bow in a smith shop?"

"A nobleman visiting the shop taught me to use the bow, sir."

Bors studied him. "I met the smith of Edenton once long ago. You don't look like him."

"Nay, sir," Rhys blurted out quickly as if he didn't want to be caught saying it.

"And what should I call you?"

"Sir?"

"Your name," Bors said impatiently. "You have a name, don't you?

"Aye, sir. 'Tis Rhys," he said with a slight, awkward bow.

Bors scratched his beard. "Well then, Rhys, I'll be riding to Iconium. Will you be coming?"

"Aye sir," Rhys agreed hastily. "I'll go with you to the abbey. Thank you, sir."

Bors climbed into the saddle and nudged the horse. The animal pranced forward at a lively pace. Bors crossed the stream and rode past two dark fir trees, disappearing from sight. Using the spear, Rhys splashed across the stream and hobbled as fast as he could toward the trees. A moment later Bors rode back around the trees. He stopped the horse and looked down at Rhys.

"I'll be a little slow," Rhys explained. "I twisted my ankle running from Acwellen's thanes."

"Ever ridden a horse?"

"Nay, sir."

"Leave the spear. You won't need it on the horse."

Rhys dropped the spear. Bors reached down and grasped Rhys' hand, lifting him off the ground and onto the back of the horse. "Hang on. I don't want to miss the brothers' evening meal and go to bed hungry."

* * *

As I followed the riders into the forest, I heard someone call my name. I turned and was relieved to see Zophar and a bronze-haired angel coming toward me.

"The man Gabriel recommended rode this way on a gray horse. Have you seen such a man?" Zophar asked.

I motioned for them to follow me. "They are on horseback; ahead of us in those trees."

The bronze-haired angel nodded to me. "I am Eleazar, guardian to this man whose name is Bors. Forgive us for coming late. Devils lurking along the road delayed us. "

I nodded my greeting to him as we passed a bend in the trail and saw the riders ahead. "Have you been Bors' guardian since his birth?"

"His previous guardian was injured ten years ago. We took him to Orion, and I've been Bors' guardian ever since. The man keeps one busy."

"Have you and Bors been to Edenton in those ten years?"

"No, but I've heard about Dragon, and Zophar told me of your mission."

"Then you know that the young man, Rhys, is unprepared. We must keep him safe while he learns the ways of the Spirit. Can we count on Bors to help Rhys?"

Eleazar frowned. "Bors tends to be guided by his own strength."

"Gabriel didn't say that Bors would be the one to teach Rhys about the Spirit," Zophar told me. "But did we not say that we needed to find someone who can show the young man who he really is?"

What Zophar said was true. It would probably be impossible to find one man who could provide everything Rhys needed to prepare for his calling as lord protector of Edenton.

Eleazar said, "Bors is impetuous, but he is long on courage and good of heart. And he would do almost anything to bring Acwellen's rule to an end. You can be sure, if he knows who this young man is, he will help him in any way he can."

"Then let us find a way to make Rhys known to him," I said.

* * *

Rhys soon found himself desperately clutching Bors' chain mail shirt to keep himself on the big gray horse. Bors seemed to not notice. He hummed, slightly off key, various melodies, some of which Rhys had heard in Edenton. Sometimes they followed a trail through the forest. Occasionally, the trees gave way, and they would ride across a small open meadow. The sun moved westward across the sky from one tall white cloud to another.

After they had ridden for several hours, Rhys asked "Do you always avoid the roads?"

"Acwellen and I had a foul parting many years ago," Bors replied. "So I avoid Edenton and the roads going in and out of it."

"What would happen if one of his thanes saw you?"

Bors thought for a moment. "Most of them would run. They be bold when they come up against commoners who are unarmed or have no interest in the fight. 'Tis a different story when they face a sword. Then they fight only if they outnumber their enemies. But I have given my word that I'll do nothing to cause tension between Acwellen and the abbey. You see, I represent the abbey to the towns and lords throughout Wessex. If I fought Acwellen's thanes, it would set Acwellen against the abbey. Neither I nor the Holy Father want that."

"The Holy Father?" Rhys asked.

"Father Wilfrid, the abbot of Iconium," Bors replied. "Have you never been to a monastery?"

"Nay, sir."

"Well, 'tis nothing like you've known in Edenton. The brothers vow to poverty and chastity. Eight times a day they gather to sing and pray. It begins after midnight with the Opus Dei. I wonder that they be not mad from lack of sleep."

"Opus Dei?"

"In the Roman's tongue, it means 'the work of God.'"

By late afternoon, the horse and riders left the forest for a road that climbed a broad, open rise. From the top of the incline, Rhys saw down the road before them a stone wall as high as a man's head. Inside the wall were a number of stone and wood buildings. One he recognized as a chapel with its tall, thatched roof and crowned with a wooden cross. An open courtyard lay between the chapel and several long, low buildings.

"Be that the abbey?"

Bors nodded. "It began as a chapel. The brothers added the dorter, the long building where they sleep. Then they added the scriptorium, where they copy the manuscripts. The refectory be where they eat, and the little building on the other side of the courtyard be the stable."

Beyond the abbey several rows of cottages were surrounded by meadows and fields. The village looked like Edenton, only spread out more and with an abbey instead of a lord's manor. They took the road that led down to the abbey.

"I must pay a visit to an old friend before we reach the abbey," Bors said.

He stopped the horse at the entrance to a small cemetery of white crosses and white washed stones. Bors waited for Rhys to dismount the horse. Rhys himself was eager to be back on the ground, but was not sure how to get there. He finally slid off the rear of the horse and landed on his backside. The big gray horse stepped forward nervously. Bors reigned the horse and patted its mane before dismounting and tying the reins to a low hanging branch on a cherry tree. He walked past several new graves with piles of fresh earth and clean white crosses. At a small weathered cross in the back of the cemetery, he stopped. Rhys watched him sigh, lower his head, and close his eyes. Rhys' recalled the day Ormod's wife was buried in the Edenton cemetery—he still thought of her as his mother. He surveyed the weathered crosses and wondered who these people had been and what had happened to them.

Bors began to speak softly. He opened his eyes and seemed to be addressing the ground in front of the cross. "I pray, dear friend, that your memory fades not before justice comes to your lands, to your daughter, to those who served and loved you. Until that day, rest in peace, my lord."

Bors turned abruptly and began walking toward his horse. Rhys limped quickly after him. "Please, sir, tell me who this man was."

Bors silently untied the horse's reins from the tree. He looked at Rhys, and Rhys saw the light had left Bors' dark eyes. "He be the lord under whom I first served as a young thane," Bors replied firmly. "He showed me mercy, showed me how to honor good, taught me to fight. And he taught that there be a time to kill."

Bor's words sent a shiver through Rhys. He sensed that Bors had said all that he cared to and wanted to be left to his thoughts. But Rhys couldn't remain silent. "Please, sir, if it would not anger you, would you tell me what happened to this lord?"

Bors' eyes narrowed under his sole eyebrow. His face tightened into a scowl. "Acwellen," he growled, turning to Rhys with a cold stare, "betrayed him. We had ridden forth from the manor to fight barbarians attacking Lord Alured, God rest him. After the battle, my lord and I left the wounded and returned to Edenton for Lady Cwen was with child. When we arrived, Acwellen was waiting with a number of hired thieves and scoundrels. My lord was killed. I escaped with his daughter, Elene."

Bors turned the big gray horse around and began to lead it along the road toward the abbey. Rhys hobbled along beside him. Bors shook his head and said "Someday…"

Rhys noticed that he had placed a hand on his sword hilt.

"…wrongs will be righted. The murder, the theft, the injustice that Acwellen has wrought on Edenton will be undone. Someday…Lord Erlan will be avenged."

# Chapter 7

## THE REVELATION

Rhys stared at Bors. "Lord Erlan? 'Tis the grave of Lord Erlan?"

"Aye" Bors said without stopping or turning around. "Erlan was lord of Edenton before you were born. God rest him."

Rhys felt his heart pounding. *Could this be the one Ormod was talking about?*

"Please forgive me if I test your patience, sir," he said. "But when was Lord Erlan killed? Be it seventeen years ago at Christ Mass?"

Bors stopped and looked back at Rhys. The gray horse shook its head impatiently and snorted.

"About fifteen years ago," Bors said slowly. "Nay…'tis seventeen years now." Bors gazed at Rhys. A thought dawned in him like the first light of day. He approached the thought directly; "How many years be you?"

"Seventeen," Rhys said.

"Before Christ Mass?"

Rhys nodded. "Seven days."

"Didn't you say your father was Ormod, the smith, in Edenton?"

Rhys looked up the road toward the trees through which they had come. *There is no turning back now*, he thought. Bors eyes were fixed upon him. "Until a few days ago, I believed so. But then Ormod said some things I didn't understand."

Rhys' face flushed red. "Ormod said I was the son of Lord Erlan. He said they had brought the lord's son to him, and he raised him as his own. Then he said that they had taken his own son, meaning Alayn, and...left me."

Bors's eyes rested on Rhys while he thought back to events that had lain fallow for years. Rhys waited, glancing down at the horse's hooves to avoid Bors' gaze. The big gray horse pawed the ground and snorted.

"Did Ormod say who brought the lord's son?"

Rhys glanced up and shook his head.

When Bors spoke next, his voice was low and distant like the sea. "I could barely keep up with Erlan when we rode back to the manor. He so badly wanted to know if Cwen had borne him a son. The moment we entered the main hall Acwellen and his men were on us. We drew our swords and, keeping our backs to one another, tried to fight our way through them. Erlan and I were so full of salt we would have fought every saint, angel, and devil from here to the sea."

Bors fell silent, contemplating that central moment.

"Alas, Erlan heard the cry of his young daughter, Elene. One of those scoundrels had taken her from her nurse. Erlan was on him like a hawk. But for a moment Erlan's back was unguarded. He got a sword wound to the back. I made the scoundrel pay for that swipe! Erlan rescued Elene, and we escaped with the nurse."

Bors sighed and cast his eyes toward the cemetery. "Erlan's wound was too deep. He died that night while we hid in the forest."

Bors turned his gaze to Rhys. "His son..." he said in a dream-like voice. "Erlan's son...could it be?"

"Sir," Rhys said, "could Ormod's words be caused by too much ale?"

Bors narrowed his eyes as he studied the young man. "When I first saw you this morning, something about you seemed familiar, though I could not say why. Now I see you have Erlan's eyes and face. As for Ormod, some men say with the drink what they would not dare to say sober."

"Who'd believe it? Lord Erlan's son...raised by a smith in the very shadow of the manor house. What'll Elene think?"

Bors caught Rhys by the shoulders and hugged him till Rhys gasped for breath. Then Bors stepped back and his smile faded. "Does anyone else know about this—whose son you be?"

"No one, unless Ormod told them. I've talked to no one, save you."

"He's kept the secret well thus far. Let's hope his lips do not loosen now that they have his son. If Acwellen knew about you, you'd be dead." Bors frowned and looked down the road toward the abbey. "It does change things, you being Erlan's lost son. Acwellen's thanes and I have kept our distance till now."

Bors took the reins of the gray horse and started toward the abbey. "Come on, Erlan's son. Can't have you going hungry."

"Sir, you mentioned a girl, Elene," Rhys said limping after Bors. "What happened to her?"

Bors rolled his eyes toward heaven. "A stubborn young woman. She lives with a farmer and his wife in Iconium. The monks have educated her as a lord's daughter should be."

"And what about Erlan's wife, the Lady Cwen?" Rhys wondered if he should ask; after all, Ormod's wife had raised him and loved him like a son.

Bors sighed and looked with pity at Rhys. "Only Acwellen and Gwendolyn know the answer to that. Elene has asked that question many times." The horse snorted and pulled on the reins to reach the grass at the side of the road. Bors pulled back. "Come on," he growled at the animal, "You'll not feed while my own belly goes waiting."

\* \* \*

We gazed upon the abbey from the cemetery road.

"As we had hoped—Rhys now knows who he is," Zophar

said. "But is Bors the one to prepare him to battle Dragon?"

"If you hope to take the manor by sword, Bors be your man. If not...." Eleazar shook his head.

We could see monks and angels moving among the abbey's stone and wood buildings. The abbey's beauty was not just a fine arrangement of stone or timber in the building walls; it was the heaven-like order and peaceful atmosphere. It was a place where angels felt at home.

Eleazar said, "Perhaps the person to guide Rhys' heart is at the abbey."

"Hibernian monks who founded the abbey at Iona were as much warriors as they were mystics," I said. "In Wessex, a monk is either one or the other, but rarely both. We need the fierce heart of a warrior and the quiet, discerning spirit of a monk."

"Who was the monk who founded Iona?" Zophar asked.

"Columcille. A flawed man but certainly a warrior. Remember the battle of Cooldrevay?" I thought about it for a bit. "We need not find the man to face Dragon. That task has been given to Rhys. We need to find the man to shape the one who faces Dragon."

\* \* \*

With Rhys at his side, Bors led the gray horse down the road to the abbey gate. He told Rhys how the lord who had once owned the land had died with no heirs, so he gave the lands with the chapel to monks of the Benedictine order. Father Wilfrid was now the abbot and oversaw the abbey as well as the surrounding lands that belonged to the abbey.

The abbey's heavy oak gates were open. Rhys saw that between the buildings was a stone courtyard surrounded by flowers and gardens. They passed the stone chapel and came to a small wooden gate that opened into a fenced yard. The yard held several dozen sheep along with four brown cows. At the far end of the yard was a small stable. It was to the stable that Bors led the horse. The stable had walls on three sides but was open on the fourth. The thatch roof was just high enough for Bors to stand up straight.

Bors said, "Since you've never been to an abbey before, it'll be a little odd for you. Watch what I do. There be only certain times and places in which the brothers are permitted to speak. Until you learn what to do, do not speak unless spoken to."

Rhys nodded.

"You've got it already!" Bors grinned.


They left the horse in the fenced yard with the sheep and the cows. Rhys followed Bors through the small gate and across the courtyard.

A man approached them from the other side of the courtyard. He was younger than Bors but at least a dozen years older than Rhys. The top of his head was shaved so that a ring of hair from ear to ear remained. He wore a plain black tunic covered by a sleeveless garment, or cowl, with a deep hood in the back. As he neared, he looked at them and nodded. Bors nodded back. Rhys stopped, watching the monk and waiting for him to speak. But the monk dropped his eyes and continued past them silently. Bors was nearly across the courtyard when he realized Rhys was not behind him. He turned to see Rhys gazing at the monk. Bors raised his eyebrow and waited.

Rhys turned and quickly walked across the courtyard. His face flushed red. He started, "Sorry, sir..." But Bors raised his hand to silence Rhys.

Across the courtyard and behind the refectory were several smaller buildings and a large herb garden. There were gardens in Edenton, but none as large and colorful as this. It had purple, yellow, and blue plants; some were flowers, others looked like weeds. Rhys recognized some of the plants, but did not know their names or what they were used for. They approached two men who were carefully inspecting a plant held by the younger of the two. A rook, black as night, hopped sideways on the younger monk's shoulder. It cocked its head to the side and stared at Rhys. Rhys could hear the older monk ask, "What is the plant's purpose?"

The younger monk replied, "It provokes urine and stays the fluxes of the belly."

The older man pointed to a yellow flower. "Cankerwort," the younger man said. "The juice makes a poultice and cleanser for wounds, aching joints, and burns."

The older man bent down and plucked a thistle from among the cankerwort. "We must not tolerate weeds," he admonished.

The younger man looked at him coldly and said, "Sow-thistle, Holy Father. The leaves may be used in porridge. It may also be used to treat fevers, stones, deafness, and swelling."

The older man looked down at the thistle he had been about to pitch. "Fevers, eh?" he said, handing it to the younger monk. "Give it to the brothers in the kitchen for the porridge."

The younger man bowed. "Aye, Father." He glanced at Bors and nodded to him as he left. The older man turned to see who it was behind him. He smiled warmly through green eyes. "Brother Bors," he said. "You have returned!"

From his ring of gray hair and the pale, wrinkled face, Rhys judged him to be about the same age as Bors. He was nearly Bors' height, but slightly built. He bowed deeply.

Bors bowed as well. "Abbot Wilfrid," he replied in a low voice, "inspecting the herb garden?"

"We've added herbs to supply the infirmary, and we must learn about them," explained the abbot. "Shall we meet in the scriptorium? I'll instruct the brothers in the kitchen to add a place for you and your friend at the table." He smiled at Rhys and bowed again.

Bors returned a half bow, which Rhys awkwardly tried to imitate. Rhys followed Bors to the scriptorium. It was a tall, rectangular building, similar to the chapel, but made from timbers rather than stone. Inside the scriptorium, Rhys noted three rows of tall desks, two rows on the left and one row on the right, with an aisle in between. Quill pens and parchment rolls lay on each desk, surrounded by various colored ink bottles and candles. A tall wooden stool stood next to each desk.

Bors pulled two stools to the nearest desk and settled on one of them. "Abbot Wilfrid is a good host," he announced merrily.

"Do you live here?" Rhys asked.

"Only a week or two at a time. Then I travel to a town or manor to conduct the business of the abbey. The monks make wool and parchment and copy manuscripts. When the business be done, I return for another week or so. Iconium and the abbey only need someone now and then to act as the town reeve. That be what I do when I come here. Not like Acwellen in Edenton. He needs a reeve worse, since there be many who hate him."

Abbot Wilfrid entered the scriptorium. He pulled a stool to the front of the desk and sat across from Bors and Rhys. He took a deep breath before smiling. "We have a little time before the meal. Would you do me the kindness, Bors, of introducing me to your friend?"

Bors motioned to Rhys, "I met Rhys on the road to Iconium—the son of an old friend. Acwellen's thanes caught him and his friend hunting on freemen's land and accused them of poaching. They got his friend, but Rhys escaped them."

Rhys winced inwardly at Bors' mention of the poaching incident.

Abbot Wilfrid smiled hesitantly at Rhys and said, "Well, Rhys, welcome to the abbey at Iconium."

Rhys attempted a smile even as the abbot's faded quickly. "You had no incident with Acwellen's guard, I pray." he said to Bors.

"I took the forest trail. Didn't see a single one of them."

"Could they be following you?" Abbot Wilfrid asked with a glance toward Rhys.

Bors shook his head. "He was hiding in the cave along the trail between here and Edenton. They'll not stray too far from the road unless they see someone. It's unlikely that they found his trail."

The abbot shifted on his stool and took a deep breath. "We just don't want any conflict with Lord Acwellen. You cannot dwell on your past disagreements. Do you understand that Bors?"

Bors turned his head slightly, raised his eyebrow, and studied Wilfrid. "Have I ever done anything to endanger the abbey, Holy Father?"

"Nay. But I worry about your hatred for Lord Acwellen. We must do everything we can to keep the peace with him."

Bors did not reply to the abbot; they sat for a moment in awkward silence. Finally, Bors cleared his throat. "Have there been any problems in the village?"

Abbot Wilfrid shook his head. "The miller's son got drunk and started a fight with the son of Aldred. But the miller found him and switched him sore. I think the young man was full of regrets when he sobered."

Bors chuckled, "It'll be many a day before he tries that again, I would guess."

"Did you find Lord Eadmund well?" the abbot asked Bors, "Has he seen any raiders along the sea coast?"

"No raiders this year," Bors replied. "But I need to see Brother Carlyle—to see how he comes with the lord's manuscript. Lord Eadmund eagerly awaits it."

Abbot Wilfrid frowned and rubbed the lines on his forehead. "Brother Carlyle's not here," he said softly.

Bors raised his eyebrow and leaned over the desk. "Not here? Where be he?"

"He's gone to the abbey cottage in the forest, beyond the great ash tree on the hill northeast of the abbey. He was restless. I thought it would be good for him to be alone, away from the distractions."

Bors' eyes narrowed in a questioning gaze.

"Even the abbey has distractions," the abbot continued. "He left about three weeks ago. I have not heard from him since he left."

Bors sat up and folded his arms. "Did he give you a reason for his being restless?"

"He had a vision," Abbot Wilfrid said.

"Of the blessed Mother?"

The abbot shook his head, frowning. "Nay." He looked Bors in the eye and paused; clearly, the subject was not to his liking. "He saw a vision of the abbey burning."

"On fire?"

"Aye. A fire ignited by the breath of a dragon."

Bors rubbed his chin. "I've heard of visions of the blessed Mother or the wounds on our Lord's hands. But I've never heard of a vision of an abbey on fire."

Abbot Wilfrid glanced momentarily at Rhys, before telling Bors, "The monks who established the monastery at Iona were trained in the use of weapons. Since their time, Iona and many other monasteries have been overrun by raiders. Brother Carlyle thinks we should arm and train the monks to defend this abbey in the case of an attack. The issue came to a head when he had the vision of the abbey burning."

"He wants you to arm the brothers?"

The abbot nodded. "Carlyle's own father was a thane for a lord in the land of Hibernia. He learned to fight, use a sword, and a bow. I've often wondered if he regrets having left that life for one of devotion to the spiritual disciplines."

"And so your disagreement led to this restlessness?" Bors asked.

"He came to me with the request that we order arms. I refused. I told him that we must follow the traditions of the Benedictine brothers and trust God. He said that not all traditions were passive in the face of evil."

"So you sent him away?"

Abbot Wilfrid sighed. "I tried to convince him of the folly of his position, but it was no use. We could not have dissention or conflict at the abbey."

A monk appeared and motioned to Abbot Wilfrid and then left. The abbot nodded and said, "Our supper is ready."

Bors told Rhys, "I need to speak to Abbot Wilfrid alone.

Go ahead to the refectory. We'll meet you there in a moment."

Bors waited till Rhys left, then spoke to the abbot. "Lord Eadmund awaits his manuscript. And now I need to go in search of Carlyle." Bors paused before saying, "I had hoped to leave Rhys here."

Abbot Wilfrid rubbed his right hand across the table for a moment. "You know, Bors, we welcome anyone here who has need...under normal circumstances. But a fugitive from Lord Acwellen could endanger the abbey. I'm not sure that would be wise."

"Acwellen be a thief and a murderer," Bors said. "There has only been peace with him because the abbey has nothing he wants. If he changes his mind, if he decides he wants to rule Iconium or the abbey, the peace will end. Then, as Brother Carlyle says, you'll have to defend yourselves or become his servants."

"Bors, 'tis the very reason why I am hesitant for Rhys to stay here. I would prefer to avoid conflict with Lord Acwellen by making sure there is nothing here he wants, including Rhys." Abbot Wilfrid stood. "Let's not keep the brothers waiting. We shall discuss it tomorrow."

\* \* \*

The abbey guardian, an angel named Mythiel, was patient and kind, though he had fought few battles. When Abbot Wilfrid mentioned Carlyle's vision, I asked Mythiel, "Of Carlyle and this vision, what knowledge have you?"

"The heavens have not spoken. Whether this dragon be Edenton's dragon or signify raiders from the north, or the vision simply be Carlyle's imagination, I know not."

"For certain, I see this vision as a warning," Zophar said. "What will happen if there comes an onslaught?"

Mythiel smiled feebly. "I have set guards, but vigilance is hard to keep. Never has the abbey been attacked. The devils we see here use not swords but words and thoughts. Some of the angels have stopped carrying swords. Furthermore, Abbot Wilfrid does not believe in such defense. Even if we guard against spirits of darkness, it will not be enough if the monks are not vigilant against men such as Acwellen."

To Mythiel I said, "Many seasons we have watched Dragon. Be aware that he kills all those that threaten his power. He fears the Spirit most of all—and anyone the Spirit sends. Vigilance be required, Mythiel."

"Acwellen's thanes are on the hunt for Rhys," Zophar added. "They may follow him here."

\* \* \*

Rhys wandered across the courtyard and wondered if the two men were talking about what to do with him. He had thought that the abbey would be a place of refuge for him. Now that he was here, everything seemed so strange. *Why couldn't I stay with Bors?* he thought.

A moment later the two men appeared. Neither smiled nor spoke to him. He followed them into the refectory. Rhys sat next to Bors at the end of a long table of monks. No one spoke. The only sound was the scuffing of the monks' brogues on the floor. Several monks entered the room carrying chunks of dried bread covered with boiled potatoes and cabbage. The smell of the potatoes made Rhys' head feel light. The waiting was torture. He closed his eyes to try to block the food out of his mind. When he opened his eyes again, he noticed Bors smiling and nodding at the monk who brought the food. Then Wilfrid stood, the monks bowed their heads, and he asked a blessing on the meal.

When the prayer ended, Rhys snatched up a potato and stuffed it into his mouth. As he chewed, he glanced about and noticed something odd. One of the monks was waving his hands in front of him as the monk across the table watched. Then the first monk stopped and the second monk began to wave his hands in odd motions in front of him. Rhys realized that these monks were talking to one another through their hand motions. Monks throughout the room were waving their hands or watching others waving to them. Bors, concentrating on his potatoes and cabbage, seemed to not notice. Rhys picked up another potato, took a bite, and gazed at the odd looking spectacle around him.

# Chapter 8

## FLEEING THE ABBEY

Rhys had never seen anyone use sign language, let alone a roomful of silent monks eating and signing at the same time. He watched, astonished. Bors stood suddenly, and all eyes turned toward him. He bowed, a sort of after-dinner thank you. The brothers nodded and smiled back at him. Rhys rose quickly to follow Bors, bowing clumsily as he stood. His face reddened as he sensed the silent stares. But he did not want to be left behind in a room of silently waving, nodding men. Bors would talk to him and, at the moment, Rhys took great comfort in that.

Rhys followed Bors across the courtyard to the stable. Darkness and the smell of hay welcomed them as they entered. They saw the backside of the gray horse as it ate from a wood trough on the far wall. Bors spoke to the animal and patted its neck. "I see the brothers gave you hay. Not like the wild grass along the trail, but it tastes good now and then, eh?"

Bors reached under the trough and pulled out two three-legged milking stools. He handed one to Rhys. The other he placed next to the wooden trough. Bors sat on the stool, leaning back against the stable wall and stretching his legs out in front of him. "Behold, the great hall of the manor house for such a wayfaring man!" he said, grinning.

Bors turned to Rhys and said in a low voice, "I have known Brother Carlyle for nearly ten years. He has always been a little different than the other monks at Iconium."

Rhys thought back to the abbot's description of Carlyle's vision. "Might he have been drunk?"

Bors cried, "Hah! Carlyle drunk?" At the sudden sound, the gray horse raised its head and stared at the man. Bors remembered himself, quieted, and looked about the stable. He said in a restrained tone, "A more serious man I've not met. I've not seen him laughing, let alone drunk." Bors snorted a couple times and smiled to himself.

The two fell silent, watching darkness gather outside the stable. After a time, Rhys said, "Sir, since you knew Lord Erlan and Lady Cwen, will you tell me about them?"

Bors sighed. "So you want to hear the stories? I told Elene everything I could remember from those days—hunts, feasts, harvests, and festivals. Not that women want to hear about battles, but I told her about those too."

He sat brooding for a moment. "Tomorrow we'll go to see Elene. Maybe I'll tell you some of the stories then. She'll help my memory, lest I forget something; she has heard them enough to tell you herself."

Rhys nodded.

Bors cleared his throat. "The brothers' company be strange, but their hospitality be true. Even so, I often sit with the animals. I don't want to interrupt their prayers." Bors rubbed his beard. "You may want to think on that," he said. "In case you be here for a while."

Rhys' heart sank. "Can't I travel with you? If I had a bow, I could hunt for meat. And I wouldn't get in the way. The brothers' ways be strange to me. They keep waving their hands and nodding."

Bors rocked forward on his stool long enough to rub his lower back. "I've talked to Abbot Wilfrid about it," he said. "But he has not yet given me an answer. If he agrees, you'll stay here, at least while I search for Carlyle and go back to Lord Eadmund's manor. Elene has agreed to be a tutor and nanny for Lord Eadmund's daughter. My plan was to take her and the manuscript at the same time. But with Carlyle gone, who knows? Acwellen's thanes'll be looking for you. If they find us, I couldn't protect both you and Elene. You'll stay here, if it be acceptable with Abbot Wilfrid."

"But if I had a bow, I could help if there was a fight."

"Nay. If the abbot agrees, you'll stay here."

Rhys wanted to argue, but he could see that Bors' mind was made up.

"We'll leave within the week. The abbot and I have more business to discuss first," Bors said.

"And Elene?"

"We'll see her tomorrow. She must be told that she has a brother. Not sure what she'll say—strong-headed lass."

Suddenly they heard footsteps approaching the stable. A monk came to the door and peered in at them.

"Good evening, brothers," he said.

Bors replied, "Good evening, brother. Evening prayers done?"

"Aye. I've come to show you to your rest."

"Ah," Bors said, rising to his feet. "Too many nights have passed since I slept on a straw mat. Lead on."

The monk led them across the dark courtyard to the dorter. It was a long building with rows of straw mats lying down both sides of the room. Here and there one could see the form of a monk lying on a mat. They walked quietly to the other end of the room. The monk pointed to two mats. Bors smiled and nodded. As soon as the monk left, Bors stripped off his tunic, lay down on the mat in his linen undergarments, and pulled the blanket over him. A moment later, he was snoring.

Rhys was tired, but too many things crowded into his head. He took off his tunic and lay on the mat next to the wall. Pulling the blanket over him, he stared up at the ceiling. He thought of Bors and the monks, Ormod, and Alayn. He thought of how big the world was outside of Edenton. And all the time he was growing up it was there, and he wondered that he hadn't known it.

* * *

Though the abbey angels did not keep a regular watch over the abbey at night, Zophar, Eleazar, and I agreed we would take turns standing watch. I took the first watch. After dark fell, I climbed up on the abbey wall and walked along it, turning my gaze first toward the town, then the surrounding forest, and finally the road to Edenton for signs of devils. The moon rose and lined the clouds in silver light.

A little after midnight, Eleazar came out of the dorter to take over the watch. He climbed onto the wall near the abbey gate facing the cemetery.

"Any signs of danger?" he asked.

"None. Only the clouds and the moon, occasionally."

I saw a star winking between clouds. "Eleazar, did you ever meet an angel named Zorran? Before the rebellion, I mean."

Eleazar shook his head.

"He was a friend before the fall. Our paths crossed again at the start of this mission. He was guarding Edenton for Dragon. I had to enter Edenton, and so we had a sword fight. I sent my friend, my former friend anyway, to hell that night. But there was nothing else I could do; he wouldn't let me enter, and that was my task."

"You had no choice, Iothiel."

"I had no choice," I agreed. "But he had been a friend…. Do you ever think about them, Eleazar: all those angels who fell from the heavens? Do you wonder if we can do anything to restore them?"

Eleazar studied me for a moment. "Do you remember that day, Iothiel? A decision was made by every created angel—follow and serve God or rebel and follow the archangel, Lucifer. Those angels turned away from the very one that created them. They wanted the glory that the Creator gave to the man and woman. That's why we stand guard over these mortals even now."

He looked out into the darkness. "You ask if I think about

trying to restore them; I do not. That's not my mission. When you are trading sword blows with one of those devils, a thought like that may cause hesitation. And the one who hesitates in battle loses."

I drew a deep breath and stared out into the darkness in front of the abbey as clouds slipped across the sky. I thought about what Eleazar said about his mission, and I thought of my own mission—whether I had served it as well as I was capable. Then, a movement near the cemetery caught my attention. I waited, wondering if the movement had been my imagination. A moment later, another shadow flitted through the moonlight.

"Did you see that?" I asked Eleazar.

He nodded, "Do you think it's more than a stray devil?"

"There is something else," I said, pointing at the horizon just beyond the road from Edenton. There was a patch of light coming from just over the hill, and it was moving toward the abbey.

"A night raid?"

"Riders from Edenton carrying torches is my guess," I said. "Are the monks still at their midnight prayers?"

"Midnight prayers ended half an hour ago. I believe they've all returned to their sleep."

"Find a way to awaken Wilfrid quickly," I told Eleazar. "We need to get someone in the abbey moving while we find out who is coming."

\* \* \*

Rhys rolled over and opened his eyes, trying to remember why he was sleeping in the long, dark room.

"Rhys!"

Bors stood over him, fully dressed with his chain mail over his tunic. Bor's scabbard and sword hung at his side. "Get up, Rhys!" he whispered. "We must go now! The reeve of Edenton be here looking for you."

The sleep lifted suddenly from Rhys' mind. He pushed the

blanket off, sat up, and began pulling on his tunic. "He be here?" Rhys asked.

Bors waved his hand impatiently. "Come!"

Rhys followed Bors out the side door of the dorter, hobbling to keep up as they crossed the courtyard. The damp night air was lit only by moonlight. Rhys heard men's voices, snorting horses, and creaking saddles coming from beyond the abbey gate. A monk stood in the dark stable, holding the gray horse by the reins. Bors took the reins and led the animal outside the building. He quickly mounted the horse and held his arm out for Rhys. Rhys made an awkward attempt to climb on the back of the horse. Bors pulled and the monk gave a push from behind. Rhys was barely on when Bors nudged the horse's sides, and they moved away from the stable. They rode along the wall to the back of the abbey, where another monk appeared from the shadows and opened a narrow gate that was mostly hidden by thick-growing vines.

Rhys turned and saw the gate close behind them. The stone wall, black in the moonlit night, formed the back of the abbey. Rhys wondered if the men at the abbey's gate would soon be coming through the back gate after them. Bors guided the horse into a stand of trees and then turned toward the town.

"I didn't think Acwellen's thanes would come," Bors said. "'Tis fortunate, Abbot Wilfrid did not sleep well. He was in the refectory when he saw them ride past the cemetery—their torches gave them away. He woke me immediately and planned our exit. If there be one thing I'll say for those brothers, they manage well."

"How did he know they were looking for me?"

"Who else would they be looking for? Methinks they may know who you be."

Rhys imagined Father Wilfrid facing Acwellen's thanes by torchlight in front of the abbey. "Do you think Acwellen's thanes will kill the abbot or any of the monks?"

Bors shook his head. "The abbey has always been on peaceful terms with Acwellen even though he has not supported the abbey or the Church. I don't know what purpose it would serve him to attack the abbey."

They rode along a line of trees to the edge of a small meadow next to the cottages of Iconium before Bors turned the horse onto a road that led into the village.

"I won't be staying at the abbey then?" Rhys asked.

Bors didn't answer, but Rhys heard the low snorting of a horse. Beyond several dark trees ahead, he saw the outline of the animal. He heard voices saying goodbye. Next to the horse he saw the outline of a long-haired woman embrace a smaller, round-shaped woman and a thin man. Bors reigned up the gray horse. He said in a quiet voice, "Forgive us for the hurry. But Acwellen's thanes be at the abbey."

The long-haired woman was dressed in a man's leggings and tunic. She mounted her horse with a grace that made Rhys envious.

"I suppose this is Acwellen's fugitive riding with you." she said.

Bors nodded in reply. "And bearing the image of your father, God rest him. Rhys here be your long lost brother, I suppose."

The older woman gave a startled gasp. Though the mortals could not see it in the dark, Rhys' face flushed red. Neither could Rhys see the reaction on Elene's face. She was silent for a moment. Then she turned to the older couple. "Goodbye. I'll not forget you," she said quietly, but firmly. The older woman began to sob softly.

"Don't worry," Bors told them. "She'll be safe at Lord Eadmund's manor. Now, we've got to go. We'll need to stay ahead of the thanes."

Rhys turned and looked back toward the abbey. He almost expected to see the thanes coming out of the back gate like bees pouring out of a hive. But he saw only the abbey walls, still and silent in the dark.

The man mumbled something that Rhys could not understand. The woman sniffled and blew her nose. Bors pulled on the reins of the horse, and it turned back toward the trees. Elene nudged her horse after them. They rode at a quick pace along the edge of the trees till they came to a road. There was just enough light through the trees for the horses to walk at a steady pace. Rhys started to speak, but Bors raised his finger to his lips to silence him. Rhys realized that Bors was listening for the thanes' horses.

Bors turned the horse off the road at an opening in the trees that led to a trail. As they rode, the night began to fade. The dark forms around them began to take the shape of trees; first in various shades of gray, then with brown or gray or white bark and green leaves. The harrumphing of bullfrogs and chorus of crickets hushed as the darkness lifted. Then the first light of the new sun washed through the trees bringing the chirping, cries, squawks, and songs of jays, sparrows, thrushes, and doves.

Suddenly, while stepping over a branch lying across the path, the gray horse stumbled. Rhys fell against Bors. The horse regained its footing and stopped. Bors slid off the horse and motioned for Rhys to do the same. The horse lowered its head and snorted.

"We've escaped them, at least for now," Bors said. "We'll take a moment to rest the animals."

Rhys looked at the young woman who might be his sister. She had long, wavy hair and dark eyes. Her skin was fair, and her nose was straight, much like Rhys'. It gave her a look of strength. And her cold glance at Rhys did nothing to soften her image. Rhys realized he had been staring. His face reddened as he quickly turned back to Bors.

Elene slid off her horse and led it across the ditch. "May I speak with you alone, Bors?"

Bors was inspecting the gray horse's front legs. He stood up and looked at Elene. She glared at him.

"Rhys, hold onto these horses and keep an eye out for riders," Bors said, handing his reins to Rhys. Elene handed Rhys her reins also, but she refused to look him in the face. Bors followed Elene a few paces up the path.

Rhys let the horses graze. He looked back down the dark path they had come on, watching for riders. But his mind was on the conversation taking place behind him. Rhys heard Elene's voice rising in anger. He glanced back and saw Elene pointing her finger at Bors. Bors stood listening to her with his arms folded across his chest. Elene stopped and Rhys heard Bors say, "Did I not tell you...." Then Bors lowered his voice, and Rhys could hear no more. Elene said something in reply but the only words he could understand were "stranger" and "vagabond." Rhys bit his lower lip and looked back down the path they had come. He was suddenly ashamed of his ragged appearance. His coarse tunic was stained black in spots from coal dust and had holes in the elbows. He licked his palms and tried to wipe his face clean.

A moment later Bors stood next to him. Bors took the reins of the horse and rubbed its mane. "The old horse be tired. Taking us to Iconium was enough for him." Bors turned to Rhys, "Ride with Elene for now. Her horse be fresh, and her weight be little."

Elene glared at Bors, though he didn't seem to notice. Rhys protested desperately, "I'll walk! My ankle be fine now. No need to tire out Elene's horse."

Bors untied the leather pouch holding Elene's belongings from the back of her horse and carried it to his own. "Do you think that Elene be too heavy for you to ride with her?"

"Of course not, but...."

"Well, then, up with you on the horse. Your hobbling would slow us down. Want the reeve catching up with us, do you?"

"Nay," Rhys said firmly. "I'll not impose upon the lady."

Elene mounted the horse. She looked down at Rhys impatiently, "Oh, get on! Bors'll not let it rest until you do."

Rhys looked at Bors who simply nodded at him. He sighed and reached up to the saddle to try to pull himself on the back of the horse. Bors gave him a boost, and Rhys was on. He sat awkwardly behind Elene. She turned her head slightly toward him and said curtly, "Just remember, I am said to be your sister."

# Chapter 9

## THE GRIM HILL

Rhys tried to keep his distance from Elene, but found himself being jostled to the middle of the horse. He didn't have Bors' chain mail shirt to hold on to, so he gripped the back of the saddle. His fingers soon ached, and he nearly fell off a time or two. Elene's natural grace on the horse only made Rhys' awkwardness more humiliating.

No one spoke. Bors kept his eyes on the trail. Rhys wanted to say something to Elene, to assure her that he was not lying about the things Ormod had told him, but he didn't know how to say it. So they rode in silence, frequently bowing their heads to avoid the tree limbs that hung low over the narrow trail.

When the sun was overhead, Bors stopped at a stream to water and rest the horses. He took some bread and cheese from a pouch the brothers had given him and passed it to the others. As they ate, Bors studied a piece of parchment he took from a pocket in his tunic.

"There was a path just before that last bend," Elene said. "How do you know that wasn't the way to Carlyle's cottage?"

Bors did not look up or respond.

"How far is it?" she asked.

"Father Wilfrid thought it be a day's ride."

"Can you tell where we are by the map?"

Bors got up and walked over to the gray horse. He rubbed the horse's neck. "They've had enough rest."

They mounted and continued riding, stopping only when paths converged, so Bors could study the map. The sun was setting when the path straightened, and the travelers could see up a wooded hill before them. It took nearly ten minutes to reach the top where there was a clearing nearly as big as the courtyard at the abbey. In the middle of the clearing towered a broad ash tree.

"We'll stop to rest the horses," Bors said.

Rhys quickly slid off the back of the horse. He stretched, feeling the soreness in his legs and backside from the long ride. Bors removed Elene's leather bag from the back of his horse and let the horses graze. The three travelers sat on the ground and ate the last of the bread and cheese.

Elene looked around. "Bors, where is the path leading out of the clearing?"

Bors and Rhys looked across the clearing from the way they had come. There was no sign of a trail, only thickets of brush and trees.

"Does Carlyle's map show a path from this clearing?" Elene asked.

Bors pulled the map out of his pocket and studied it.

"Well?"

Bors shrugged. "I don't see this clearing on the map. But we should be getting close."

"We're lost, aren't we?"

Bors frowned at her. "We've not found Carlyle yet, if that be what you mean. He be one man in the middle of these woods, but we'll find him."

"Do you have any idea where?"

Ignoring Elene, Bors said to Rhys. "I don't think Carlyle's cottage could be very far from here, but it'll be dark soon. We'll stay here for the night."

He handed Rhys a leather pouch containing flint. "When it's too dark for the smoke to be seen, use this flint to build a small fire. I'll ride around below the hill here and see if I can find the path to Carlyle's cottage."

"And what about me?" Elene asked.

"You stay here. Rhys, water her horse."

Bors mounted the gray horse and rode across the clearing to the only opening in the trees and brush that he could find.

Elene turned to Rhys. "You gather the fire wood," she said crossly. "I can water my own horse."

Rhys said nothing; he noticed that Elene's jaw was clinched. Walking to the edge of the clearing to gather sticks, he wondered how soon the sky would be dark enough to hide the smoke and whether building the fire under the tree would help hide it.

\* \* \*

I stood in the clearing with Zophar and Elene's guardian, Kabriel. "Evil dwells in this place," Kabriel whispered. "It be a Grim hill, I think."

"A Grim hill?" Zophar asked. "Is this not a place where mortals worship the druid gods?

Kabriel said, "The devils trick people into worshipping them in Grim's name. On the night of a full moon, Grim's followers make sacrifices to him by hanging their victim from an ash tree such as this."

Zophar raised an eyebrow and glanced at the tree behind us.

\* \* \*

Carrying sticks and branches for the fire, Rhys stopped and looked at the clearing in the fading sunlight. It was odd to see one large tree in the middle of a clearing, like someone had planned it. The clearing reminded him of something he couldn't quite name. He placed the sticks on the side of the tree away from the path. He looked up into the far-reaching branches of the tree. The limbs were gnarled and twisted, like the hands of a very old person. A heaviness settled in Rhys' chest, making him shiver. He hoped Bors would return soon, and they could go on to Carlyle's cottage. The thought of spending the night in the clearing made him feel cold.

Elene came into the clearing leading the horse. He sensed her gaze and stammered, "Gathering firewood."

"Well, if you don't start the fire soon," she said as if talking to a servant boy, "it'll be too dark to see."

Rhys looked at the sky. "Aye. Getting dark, but Bors said to wait till...." He glanced at Elene, and she gave him a stony look.

"I'll get a few more branches, then start the fire," he said. He walked quickly back to the trees for more wood.

\* \* \*

Zophar looked about the clearing and drew his sword. Following the spirit of lightness at the abbey, the Grim hill was oppressive. The daylight seemed unnatural, as if it came from the fading light of another world. The clearing seemed to be a place where there had never been joy or laughter or peace. One could almost hear the cry of dying victims.

*Bors should not have left them here*, I thought to myself.

Kabriel saw the anxious look in Zophar's face and said, "The devils delight in deceiving the descendants of Adam and Eve into acts of devotion—the creature in God's own image turning against Him to worship His enemies."

Zophar asked what we should do.

"Be sharp with your eye and swift with your sword," I replied. "The devils cannot be far off."

\* \* \*

When Elene tied the horse to the tree, she felt a cold breeze touch her cheek. *I'll be glad for a fire tonight*, she told herself. She could see a pool of fog gathering on the path at the bottom of the hill, and the thought came to her, *A thick fog will make it difficult to find a way through the forest.*

\* \* \*

We heard voices coming from the foot of the hill near the path. I drew my sword and said quietly, "Bear in mind, our mission is to protect Rhys, not avenge what has been done on this hill."

"I'm ready to put the sword to them," Kabriel said. "But we may do better if we get Elene and Rhys off this hill."

"See to it!" I told Kabriel.

A hooded wraith followed by three large devils appeared, walking toward us through the trees. Behind them on the path came three dark-robed men, one carrying a torch and one leading a goat. The devils stopped when they saw us. They were fighting devils with powerful bodies and broadswords at their sides. Their hideously scarred faces indicated that they had been to the underworld. The wraith's face was hidden beneath the hood. It carried a scythe in its left hand. "What does this mean, you standing on this sacred hill?" demanded the wraith.

"Who claims this hill that I might know how to reply?" I asked.

"This hill belongs to Grim, god of the dead," the wraith replied. "These mortals have come here to offer their sacrifice to him and turn back his anger."

Zophar snorted his disgust, "We be not witless men, believing your wicked lies. There is only one God. He owns this and every other hill, but His name be not Grim. If you were wise, you would fall on your faces this very moment and worship Him."

The wraith raised his hand to silence Zophar. "What does it matter if Grim lives only in the minds of these mortals? Mortals have used this hill to sacrifice for generations, and that is what they have set their hearts on again today. You cannot deny them that."

"We won't stop the men from coming to sacrifice," I replied, "as long as you allow the people we guard safe passage as well.

"Safe passage be theirs," the wraith said with a nod and the hint of a grin under his hood.

Zophar turned to me and whispered, "He lies."

\* \* \*

Rhys made a mound of dry grass and propped up sticks around it. From the leather pouch that Bors gave him, he took two pieces of flint and struck them together over the grass. Sparks from the flint landed on the grass and began to glow. A wisp of smoke rose from the glowing sparks. Rhys blew softly on the grass, and a little flame appeared. Rhys fanned it till the flame grew and began to lick at the sticks.

Suddenly Elene was next to him, stomping on the flame with her brogue. "What?" Rhys cried. Elene pressed her finger to her lips and motioned toward the path. Rhys stood and looked. Near the bottom of the hill he saw men in dark robes coming. The one in front carried a torch.

Elene whispered, "We must get out of this clearing!" She ran to the tree to untie her horse. But her running frightened the horse, and it reared. The more Elene pulled on the horse's rope, the more the horse pulled away. It tried to rear again but was stopped halfway up by the taunt rope. As the horse came down, Rhys grabbed its halter and with all his strength pulled it toward the tree. The rope slackened for a single moment, and Elene was able to loosen the knot. The horse reared again, but now Rhys was able to give it more rope. "Easy, now. Easy," he said softly.

The horse settled down enough for Rhys to lead it out of the clearing. Elene snatched up the food pouch and pulled her bag of belongings behind her. But by the time Rhys reached the trees and wrapped the horse's rope around a branch, Elene was twenty yards behind him. She dropped the food pouch and tried to lift the bag of belongings. Rhys dashed back to her, took the bag, and pulled her into the trees where she slumped against a tree and gasped for breath. Rhys peered around a tree into the clearing.

"Do you…see them?" Elene gasped.

Rhys shook his head.

"I dropped…the pouch."

"Maybe they'll not see it. Do you know who they be?"

Elene shook her head. She followed Rhys' gaze into the clearing. The opening of the path began to glow with the light from the torch. A heavy man in a dark robe stepped into sight. He held the torch high and gazed across the clearing in their direction.

Elene cried, "He's looking for us! They must have seen us!"

"He's wearing a robe," Rhys said, trying to stay calm. "Maybe they come from the abbey."

They watched as the man with the torch walked a few steps in their direction. Another man appeared, smaller than the first, leading what appeared to be a goat. When Elene saw it, she placed her hand over her mouth and gasped, "They're going to sacrifice to Grim!"

"'Tis a Grim hill we be on?" Rhys asked.

"Of course! They're leading a goat at night to an ash tree on a hill. Do you know nothing about Grim?" Elene asked Rhys.

"I've not seen it, though we heard tales of Acwellen's sacrifices to Grim."

"Bloody murderer!" Elene swore hotly. "Do you know who Grim's priests sacrificed in Iconium before the brothers came?"

Rhys had heard the stories, but he didn't want to say them aloud.

"Women, mostly," she said. "Those powerless to defend themselves."

They watched as the man with the torch built a fire with the sticks Rhys had gathered. The flames leaped into the sky, lighting the clearing.

Elene said, "We need to get away from this place. Who knows what they would do if they found us."

"But what do we do about Bors? He's supposed to meet us here."

"Follow me to the bottom of the hill," Elene told Rhys. "Then we'll work our way around to the direction Bors went."

Rhys picked up the heavy leather bag with Elene's belongings and turned towards the horse. Suddenly Elene let out a piercing scream that nearly stopped Rhys' heart. In the darkness before them stood a man in a dark robe. He had a crooked nose and beady eyes as black as a badger's.

"You shouldn't have come here," the man whispered hoarsely. "You've defiled Grim's sacred place."

Elene gasped, "We didn't know!"

Rhys saw something shiny in the man's right hand—it was a knife.

"We are on our way to find a friend," Elene continued, her voice rising as her fear turned to anger. "And we don't believe in Grim, so why should we care if we have defiled his sacred place?"

"Elene," Rhys whispered.

But she wasn't listening. "What kind of god is he anyway?"

"Elene!"

She went on; her anger now a consuming flame. "Why would anyone follow a god that makes you kill the innocent to please him?"

Rhys saw the man's lips tighten in a grimace of anger. "Elene!" Rhys shouted.

The knife flashed again—this time Elene saw it too. The man lunged at her with it, but she fell back, just out of his reach, spinning away from him and falling to the ground. The man jabbed at her with his knife and, missing, stumbled forward and fell to his knees.

With all his strength, Rhys swung the leather bag in the air and brought it down on the man's head. The man collapsed and lay still.

# Chapter 10

## IN SEARCH OF CARLYLE

Elene got up, slumped against a tree, and drew a deep breath. Rhys waited a moment for his heart to stop pounding.

"You alright?" he asked. "I feared you wouldn't get out of his way in time."

Elene just shook her head and wiped her hands across her cheeks. She took another deep breath and said weakly, "I wouldn't have if you hadn't pushed me."

Rhys hadn't pushed her and didn't know what she was talking about. *She must be addled from the scare*, he thought. But there was no time to discuss it. He lifted the leather bag off the man and swung it up on the back of the horse. As he began leading the horse downhill, Elene stumbled and fell to her knees. All her strength had been spent in fear and anger.

Rhys dropped the horse's reins and helped Elene up. "Come on," he said, holding her arm. "Get on the horse."

"I can walk."

"There's no time. Get on!"

With Rhys' help, Elene pulled herself into the saddle.

"Might as well ride," Rhys went on with mock gruffness as he guided the horse down the hill, "because I wouldn't have let it rest till you did."

The cloudless sky provided moonlight, but it only fell in

patches beneath the trees. At the bottom of the hill they reached the stream where Elene had watered the horse. Rhys turned to his left and started them around the base of the hill. The darkness and the thick forest growth made the progress slow. They spent so much time trying to find a way around heavy growths of brush that Rhys began to lose his sense of direction. Weariness from the long day dulled his senses even more. He began to wonder if they were going around the hill or just wandering in circles. Elene was silent. Her eyes appeared to be closed, though she still managed to lower her head occasionally to avoid low hanging branches.

The air was cool and moist. Rhys noticed wisps of fog gathering. He stopped and blinked his eyes, trying to clear his mind. He had no idea which way to go. To his right, he heard a noise of something moving in the forest. He turned and what he saw took his breath—there in the fog twenty feet from him, Rhys saw the shape of a man standing in the moonlight watching him.

Rhys' heart raced as he felt under his belt for his hunting knife. The man did not move.

"What do you want?" Rhys asked.

"I've been looking for you."

Rhys gripped the knife handle. "Why?"

"Bors asked me to."

Rhys lessened his grip on the hunting knife. "Who are you? And what happened to Bors?

"I'm Carlyle."

"Carlyle!" cried Elene, suddenly awake. "I'm sorry I didn't recognize you. Where is Bors? Is your cottage nearby?"

"Aye. Bors will meet us there."

He stepped forward and took the reins of the horse from Rhys. He was a lean man, no taller than Rhys, with bright eyes and a white ring of hair around his shaved head.

"Follow me," he told the weary Rhys. "It'll not be far."

Their pace quickened as Carlyle led them through the forest. Still, Rhys' and Elene's weariness made the walk to the small cottage seem endless.

\* \* \*

Nothing excites devils more than the spilling of innocent blood. The devils on the Grim hill were bitterly disappointed at Elene's escape of the Grim worshipper's knife. As we followed Rhys and Elene down the hill, the devils blocked our way. Five of them, along with the hooded wraith, surrounded us. Zophar, Kabriel, and I stood back to back, facing the devils with our swords in front of us. I could barely see the wraith's sunken eyes under his hood.

"How dare you intervene in the natural order of things!" the wraith said, his voice hissing like a fire being doused with water. "She was ours, and you intervened by pushing her out of the way."

"Did you not say, 'Safe passage be theirs'?" I asked. "From your lips I heard it, and we intend to see it done whether you meant it or not."

"Tell me, then, stubborn angel—who'll protect them once we strike you down? They have escaped the Grim worshippers, but there are wolves aplenty that can do our bidding. You will not deny us the blood of innocents, for it brings us strength."

"Strength of the righteous," I told him, "comes from the blood of the Innocent One. Perhaps you can strike us down. But you will touch neither man nor woman without His permission."

The wraith screamed and raised his scythe in the air to attack us. But before he could advance, he fell and lie crumpled on the ground. Behind the fallen wraith stood an angel holding a sword in his left hand and a spear in his right. His gaze was so unyielding that I wondered how any spirit could oppose him. But the devil closest to the angel went at him to cut him down. The angel lifted the spear. With a violent motion, his arm came forward and the spear thudded into the devil's chest.

The dark forest rang with our swords as we clashed with the remaining devils. Their boldness gone, we cut down all but one which fled into the darkness.

I lowered my sword and looked to the delivering angel. "You must be Haelstrum, Carlyle's guardian. I've heard your name. I am Iothiel."

He returned my gaze, and I felt as if he was measuring me, testing the depths of my spirit. "You are the one opposing Dragon in Edenton?"

"As long as Dragon is there."

He pulled his spear out of the felled devil's chest and wiped the tip in the grass. "I find it helpful to carry two weapons when I am near a Grim hill at the time of a full moon."

I acknowledged his instruction with a nod.

Haelstrum continued, "Rhys and Elene are at the bottom of the hill. Carlyle comes this way. We should look to our charges, lest the enemy gain an advantage."

He turned and started down the hill. I walked quickly to catch up with him. "If you have heard of our mission, then you will understand our interest in Carlyle's vision of the burning of the abbey. Do you know the meaning of the vision?"

"I asked Gabriel for an interpretation, but he says the meaning of the vision rests in the hands of the Spirit alone."

"We have been fortunate to have Bors bring Rhys thus far," I told the angel. "But Bors is not the man to prepare Rhys for the battle that lies ahead. Dragon will not be vanquished by a few warriors wielding swords. From Carlyle's vision, I would assume that his heart is guided by the Spirit. Could he be the one to prepare Rhys for the battle that lies ahead?"

Haelstrum did not reply. We continued walking through the forest. I began to wonder if he had heard me when Haelstrum suddenly stopped. He nodded, and there ahead of us walked the white-haired monk. I looked at the man and thought how odd it was to be contemplating him helping to defeat Dragon.

"The vision suffers him," Haelstrum replied. "It has caused him to leave the familiar surroundings of the abbey. He has become restless and moody; his prayers vague and uncertain. At times he is not one man, but two."

"Haelstrum, we both know that those who listen to and obey the voice of the Spirit will find themselves in trying circumstances."

"True. Those devils, after all, care not if monks practice the venerating of relics. Their nightmares come from mortals who hear and obey the Spirit—for it is the Spirit who brings light to their darkness. But your question—whether Carlyle can continue under these circumstances while guiding Rhys in the ways of the Spirit—I cannot answer."

As I considered the situation, it seemed to become clear. "The way to defeat Dragon requires a man who harkens to the quiet voice of the Spirit. Many good men dwell at the abbey, though none who follows the Spirit as Carlyle has. If Rhys can learn from Carlyle the voice of the Spirit, Dragon may be defeated."

The moonlight slipped through the fog and reflected off Haelstrum's silver hair. He seemed to be considering my words. "Furthermore," I added, "we've no other choice." Haelstrum raised his eyebrows and looked at me. I forced a smile.

\* \* \*

Rhys opened his eyes the next morning as the dawn crept like smoke under the door of the small wood and mud cottage. He saw the door open; cool morning light flooded the room and then receded as the door closed. He sat up, pushed aside the wool blanket, and quietly pulled on his brogues. Outside, he found Bors leading the two horses away from the cottage. Rhys caught up with him and said good morning.

Bors glanced at Rhys. "When I returned to the camp last night, it appeared you had guests."

"'Tis a Grim hill," Rhys replied.

"I figured that out a little late. A night with a full moon brings out those Grim worshipers." Bors snorted and shook his head. "For a while there, I doubted we be finding you."

"Aye," said Rhys.

They reached the stream. Bors relaxed the horses' leads so they could lower their heads to drink. Rhys took a deep breath.

"So we found Carlyle. What do we do now?"

"Depends on his progress on Lord Eadmund's manuscript. Tis my hope that Carlyle be finished, so I may take it to Lord Eadmund. If he needs a few more days, then I shall wait here till he be finished."

"And Elene goes with you to Lord Eadmund's manor?"

Bors nodded.

"Then I stay here?"

"I haven't talked to Carlyle about that yet, but I think he will agree to let you stay till I return. As I said at the abbey," he reminded Rhys, "it is too dangerous for the three of us to travel together. And I don't want to draw Lord Eadmund into a conflict with Acwellen by asking him to harbor a fugitive."

Staring down at the stream, Rhys said quietly, "I don't want to stay here."

"If Carlyle agrees to it, you'll stay here. As I said, that be the best for everyone," Bors replied flatly.

Rhys knew that arguing with Bors would do no good. The matter was settled; he was staying here in the forest cottage with Carlyle. He would try to be grateful for Carlyle's hospitality, even if it was forced from Carlyle as well.

While Bors returned the horses to the cottage, Rhys wandered into the forest beyond the stream. He sat on a large rock and stared at the dark trees that rose from the sloping ground before him. Wind blew large white clouds across the sky. There was a sound from the direction of the cottage. Elene came walking softly through the forest. Rhys glanced around, saw her and turned away, but looked back when he realized there was something different about her. She was dressed differently; she wore an ankle-length tunic instead of men's leggings. But more than that, the cold demeanor Rhys had seen before in her was no longer there.

"May I join you?" she asked.

Rhys shrugged.

Elene stopped next to the rock that Rhys sat on and looked down the hill. For a moment, neither spoke. Then Elene said,

"Carlyle has much to do yet on the manuscript. We're leaving tomorrow for Lord Eadmund's manor."

"I'll not be going."

Elene sat down on the rock next to Rhys. "Bors told me. He would like you to go, but the risk is too great. You have to understand that."

Rhys sighed. "I don't want to stay here. I don't know what I'll do here."

"You don't know how to read, do you Rhys?"

"Smiths don't need to read."

"You're not a smith."

Rhys looked at Elene, trying to read the meaning in her face.

She went on, "When you led the horse out of the clearing on the Grim hill last night, I saw my father...I mean our father. I saw him; just like he was when I was a little girl, and he would lead the horses out of the stable behind the manor house."

"I had to help with the horses at the smith shop."

"Rhys, I'm sorry for the way I treated you. I didn't want to believe you were my brother. I thought all my family was dead. But last night I realized that you are, you must be, my brother." Elene voice faltered momentarily. "God's mercy on those who raised you Rhys, but you are not the son of a smith. You are the son of the Lord Erlan of Edenton. And a lord needs to know how to read as well as rule and fight. If you stay here, Carlyle can teach you to read."

Rhys looked down at his hands—they had failed at smithing. "Do you really believe I be your brother?"

Elene reached around Rhys' shoulders and hugged him.

Rhys' face reddened, and he felt as awkward as a boy at the May Day festival. Elene was soft and lovely and not what Rhys had imagined a sister would be. His heart pounded worse than it had when he aimed his arrow at the stag. He knew if Alayn were there, he would be mad with envy.

She leaned back and looked deeply at his face as if to remember it forever. "You are his son!" she swore. "Even though you cannot come to Lord Eadmund's manor now, I will find a way for you to come soon. Carlyle will take care of you. In the meantime, you must learn to read. That is the beginning of proper instruction for a lord."

"But why should I be instructed as a lord? I have no manor house, no lands, and no servants. I'm a peasant, barely skilled enough to smith!"

Elene's smile faded. "Rhys, your father was the Lord Erlan of Edenton. Do you not realize what that means? You are the rightful Lord of Edenton! Acwellen is a thief. He took the manor house, the lands, and the servants, but they don't belong to him."

She looked at him, waiting for the words to find their mark. "What you have, or don't have, doesn't change who you are. You are the son of Lord Erlan, and you must act like it."

She looked at him with such passion that it made him turn away. They sat silently for a moment; Elene waiting for Rhys to respond; Rhys staring at the ground. Finally, he said "I visited the manor house with Ormod to fix the iron work on the doors. That be the only thing I know of a lord and his manor."

Elene looked down the hill, focusing on something far away. "I remember mother singing to me when she lay me down at night; father taking me by the hand and leading me through the garden behind the manor house. I remember playing with my best friend, a red headed girl; the daughter of one of the servants. It was a very happy place, full of peace and joy."

A cloud passed over Elene's face as the peaceful memories came to an end. "That was before Acwellen...."

"Bors told me how Lord Erlan died."

Elene nodded and wiped a hand across her cheek. "Did he tell you about Lady Cwen, our mother?"

"He said that no one knows what happened to her."

"Someday..." Elene started. She stopped and took a breath to calm herself. "...someday I will find her, wherever she be." She sighed and rose from the rock. "Bors says that we must leave at the first light tomorrow. I must prepare."

As Elene started back to the cottage, Rhys said, "Elene..." She stopped and looked back at him. "I'll try," he said. She smiled.

\* \* \*

Eleazar came toward me through the woods. He was looking closely at me, as if trying to read my countenance. "Iothiel, we are going on tomorrow—Kabriel and I. I just heard it from Bors. He and Elene are leaving for Lord Eadmund's manor."

I gave him a nod. "Godspeed."

"But that will leave only you, Zophar, and Haelstrum. What about your mission?"

"As long as Dragon is in Edenton, our mission remains."

Eleazar gave me a tight-lipped smile. "Yes. Godspeed to you and to Edenton's freedom."

\* \* \*

The next morning, Bors woke Rhys at sunrise so he could help water the horses. They led the horses down to the stream in silence. The air was warm and moist. The early morning light spread across the sky on a blanket of clouds. As the horses drank, Bors said, "Carlyle agrees to your staying here."

"Did you tell him that I be a fugitive?"

"I told him the truth," Bors said. "Just not all of it."

"Why?"

"The threat of the sword does funny things to men. And monks be hard to read. They don't talk enough. In any case, I don't want to take the risk that he not see our side of things."

"My counsel to you," Bors continued, "be this—watch your tongue and keep your eyes to the forest for Acwellen's thanes."

Rhys' spirits dropped like a stone in a lake. He would be alone in the knowledge of who he was and in the knowledge that Acwellen's thanes might appear at any moment to take him away. And there was no telling when he would see Bors and Elene again. With a dark heart, Rhys followed Bors back to the cottage. Bors saddled the horses, and Carlyle appeared, giving Bors a leather pouch with dried pork, turnips, and a loaf of bread for their trip.

Elene emerged from the cottage with her pack. She was again wearing her riding clothes—men's leggings and the hip-length tunic. Rhys took her pack and fastened it behind her saddle. He wished they could take one last walk in the forest to talk, but Bors mounted his horse.

"It be many hours ride to Lord Eadmund's manor," he said.

Elene thanked Carlyle for his hospitality. Then she turned to Rhys. He wondered what she would say; certainly Bors would have warned Elene against giving away Rhys' identity. Elene stepped forward and kissed him on the cheek. "Remember whose son you are, Rhys," she whispered to him. She turned and mounted the horse gracefully, "Ready," she told Bors.

Bors looked hard at Rhys and told him that he would return. Rhys nodded, then turned away for the wind was causing his eyes to water.

# Chapter 11

## THE LEARNING

Rhys watched Bors and Elene till they had ridden out of sight. He waited, hoping in vain that they would return, that Bors would suddenly remember some reason why Rhys should go with them. But they did not return. A minute passed, and Rhys watched a flock of crows land in the meadow and begin searching for bugs. Carlyle had disappeared, Rhys realized. He went into the cottage, but Carlyle was not there. "Monks," Rhys muttered to himself.

The cottage, which had been empty before Carlyle's coming, had a musty smell with its log walls and hardened-earth floor. There was a wooden wash bowl, a small table with parchment and ink on it, and a small stone fireplace. Next to the wall on the far end of the room was a straw mat, for guests, and another small table with a knife, string, and a long piece of leather that appeared to be wrapped around something.

Rhys walked over to the first table and looked down at the parchment. It was nearly covered with graceful black lines and colorful drawings. A lion with a shaggy brown mane stared at him from the top of the parchment. In the middle was an angel spreading great white wings. A devil with a hideous face and bat-like wings glared at him from the bottom of the parchment.

Rhys bent over the table and placed his finger by one of the long black lines, tracing it down the thin sheet. The black lines were wide in the middle, but swept gracefully thin when curving under or over at the heights and depths. *A steady hammer and hot fire would be required for a smith to make these shapes,* he thought.

The door to the cottage creaked, and Rhys jumped. A bottle of ink flew off the table and spilled across the floor. Rhys quickly retrieved the bottle. When he looked up, he saw Carlyle.

"I've been told that you want to learn to read," he said.

"Aye, Father Carlyle," Rhys said with as much enthusiasm as he could muster.

"*Brother* Carlyle. I am a monk, not a priest."

"Aye, sir."

Carlyle moved the finished sheet of parchment to the side of the table and spread out a new, blank sheet. "I've never met a smith who had any use for reading. Do you seek a different vocation from that of your father?"

Rhys shifted his feet and glanced down at the writing on the finished parchment. He struggled to find the right words to say to Carlyle.

"Uhhhm...I've not done well in the smith shop of my...father."

It was clear by the way the monk looked at Rhys that he suspected there was something more to Rhys' story. But Rhys turned his eyes to the parchment and offered nothing more.

Carlyle said, "I am here because Father Wilfrid wanted me to be here. I am here for silence, contemplation, and prayer. I am not here to converse or listen to others converse." He waited a moment as if to let the words sink in. "However, in between the various offices of prayer, contemplation, and working on Lord Eadmund's manuscript, I'll have some moments in which I may do as I please. In those moments, I shall show you the letters that make up the words. Whether or not you learn to read is up to you."

"Aye, sir."

"In return, I've a favor to ask of you," Carlyle said.

"Aye."

"Every morning, you'll go to the hill near where I found you and Elene. Climb the ash tree at the top of the hill. From the top of the tree you can see part of the abbey at Iconium."

Carlyle's request shocked Rhys. "You want me to go to the Grim hill?"

"Aye. Have no fear. I've been there afore nearly every morning myself."

"But the worshippers of Grim were there—they saw Elene and me! One of them came at us with a knife."

"Of course they were there; it was the evening of the stag moon. There'll be no worshippers of Grim there in the mornings."

Rhys hated the thought of going back to the Grim hill, but he did not want Carlyle to think him a coward, so he did not argue. "What shall I look for?"

"For the abbey. If it's still there, come back and tell me. If it's not there, tell me that as well."

*If it's not there? How could it not be there?* Rhys wondered. He thought it a very strange request, but then everything about Carlyle seemed strange to him.

"Aye, sir," he said sullenly.

The next morning, Rhys walked back through the forest to the Grim hill. The dead goat hung from the ash tree, just as Carlyle had warned him that it would. The sight of it made him shutter. He quickly cut it down and buried it under a pile of stones. Then he climbed the tree as high as he could and looked to the southwest. He could see, as Carlyle had foretold, the steeple on the abbey chapel and the roofs of the taller buildings a day's journey away.

When Rhys got back to the cottage, Carlyle asked him what he saw. Rhys' answer seemed to satisfy the monk, for he simply nodded and motioned Rhys to the table with the parchment paper where he showed him the letter "A."

"It makes the sound of "ahh" or "a," Carlyle said, sitting on a stool next to the table.

Rhys squinted at Carlyle. "How does a letter make a sound?"

"Nay—it doesn't make the sound, you make the sound when you read it."

"Ahh or a," Rhys repeated.

"This letter is the letter "B.""

Carlyle covered half of the alphabet in the first lesson. It seemed to Rhys, the more he learned of the alphabet, the less he remembered. The next day Carlyle covered the rest of the alphabet. Rhys listened, repeated the sounds that went with the letters and tried to remember them. But it was very strange to him, trying to remember lines on a parchment. When he had learned to use the bow, he would spend hours shooting arrows at a tree, but there was no way to practice lines on a sheet of parchment.

The next day Rhys saw five deer feeding in the brush on the edge of the clearing of the Grim hill. *If I had my bow*, he thought, *Carlyle and I would have meat through the hungry season.*

Carlyle began the third reading lesson by saying, "Now that we've covered the alphabet, you can start saying the letters together for words. That is how you read."

Rhys looked at the parchment, and drew a deep breath. Carlyle pointed to a line on the parchment. "Begin here."

The first letter was tall and pointed on the top. Half-way down a line connected its two legs. Rhys recognized it and said, "Ahh."

It was followed by a little swirling line. Rhys stared at it. He knew they had covered it yesterday, but he could not remember the sound. "Ahh," he said again trying to remember the sound of the swirling letter. Carlyle pointed to the swirling letter and looked at Rhys. Rhys stared silently at the letter.

"Ess," Carlyle said.

"Ess," Rhys repeated.

"Together. Say them together."

"Ess…ahh," Rhys said.

Carlyle pointed at the first letter. "This one is first. Say it first."

"Ahh."

Carlyle pointed at the second letter.

"Ess."

"*Together*. Say them *together*."

Rhys felt as if he were back in the smith shop, trying to pound a piece of iron into the perfect shape before it cooled, with Ormod yelling instructions at him and cursing him.

"Ahh-ess."

"As," Carlyle sighed. "The word is 'as.'" He pointed to the next word. "Do you remember any of these letters?"

Rhys pointed at the first letter of the second word. "F?" he asked.

"'T,' not 'F.' It's sound is 'tuh.'"

The two stared in silent frustration at the parchment. Rhys shifted on his feet and leaned against the table.

"I wonder, Rhys, if you really want to read."

Rhys looked up from the parchment. "Why should I? Reading be for lords and monks."

Carlyle pulled on his chin. "These words that I am trying to teach you—it says, 'As the deer pants for the water, so my soul longs for You.'"

"You said you're not a smith, like your father." Carlyle waited for a response, but none came. "You don't want to read…." Carlyle paused again. "What *do* you want? What do you *long* for?"

It was a question that Rhys had never considered. Ormod had ridiculed his boyish dreams of fighting monsters as Beowulf did or killing raiders; the smith called them a foolish waste of time. And as the boy became a young man, he had nothing to replace those dreams with, except hunting with the bow. Now, with the bow broken, even that was gone.

After a long silence, Rhys said the only thing that came to him. "I know…how…to hunt."

"Do you have a spear?"

Rhys shook his head, hoping that the subject would drop. But Carlyle waited silently for more.

"I had a bow, but it got broken."

Carlyle's eyes narrowed. "A bow? Where did you get a bow?"

"A nobleman visited the smith shop and taught me to use the bow. He gave it to me. But I hit my head on a tree limb when hunting and fell on it and broke it."

Carlyle leaned back and pulled on his chin while a bee buzzed curiously around the open door. Rhys knew that he had said more than Bors' would have approved, but he didn't care. Bors had gone away and left him here, and Rhys would say what he pleased. Carlyle straightened the parchment on the table thoughtfully. He went to the door and glanced about outside, then closed the door quietly as if to keep the bee from hearing him tell a secret.

Carlyle crossed the room to the small table. "I want to show you something," he said, unrolling the long piece of leather. There were two items in the leather wrap. The first Rhys recognized as a broadsword, three feet long in a finely wrought scabbard. From the detail, he could see that it was well crafted, a sword made for a lord by a master smith. But it was the other item that Carlyle handed to Rhys. It was a piece of wood, longer and thinner than the sword, like the shaft of his old bow.

"Tell me, sir, what this wood be."

"A yew branch. Or, the shaft of a bow. I cut it from a tree I passed on the way here. It was too good a branch to pass up. I've been letting it dry. 'Tis ready to be shaped into a bow."

"You know how to make bows?"

Carlyle nodded. "My father taught me before I became a monk. This sword was his."

"I'd like to see how you make a bow."

"Perhaps we've found something you long for then. If that be the case, I'll show you how to make the bow as long as you give it a go learning how to read."

A smile slowly crossed Rhys' face.

By the end of the next week, Rhys could say all the letters of the alphabet and had begun to sound out some words. Following the reading lesson, Carlyle would take a few minutes to show Rhys how to shape the wooden shaft into a bow and cut notches on the end for the string.

The Lord's Day was the only day they did not have a lesson. Both Carlyle and Rhys went into the forest on the morning of the Lord' Day. Rhys went to the Grim hill. Carlyle went to pray.

In the sanctuary of trees, Carlyle turned his heart heavenward through hymns, prayers, and psalms. He bent his knees and turned his face to the ground in silence. Birds chirped and moments passed. Carlyle raised his face and recited the 63rd Psalm.

> *"O God, thou art my God; early will I seek thee: my soul thirsts for thee, my flesh longs for thee in a dry and thirsty land, where no water is…My soul follows hard after thee: thy right hand upholds me…But the king shall rejoice in God; every one that swears by him shall glory: but the mouth of them that speak lies shall be stopped."*

Carlyle stood and placed his hand on a tree. The final words of the psalm came back to him.

> *"…but the mouth of them that speak lies shall be stopped."*

He wandered from the woods into the garden where he frowned and plucked a few weeds from around the onion stalks. Dark storm clouds gathered overhead, but Carlyle didn't notice. *I must finish the manuscript*, he told himself as he tried to still a sudden sense of urgency. But a quiet voice spoke to him,

"That's not what I want you to do."

Carlyle stopped weeding and stared at the onion stalks in front of him. *What? How could that be? I'm not to finish the manuscript?*

"That's not what I want you to do," the voice repeated.

*But I've been working on it for months. It's been my very life! How could I have missed Your guidance? I've been faithful to everything You've asked me to do!*

"That was yesterday. Today I have something different for you. Instead of writing on parchment, I want you to make your letters on a human heart."

Had Carlyle not spent years listening to the Voice, he would not have believed what he heard. But he knew the Voice. And he knew that it was not his own voice, for he would never have made up such a shocking thought. "Aye, and whose heart would that be?" Carlyle asked, taking a deep breath to steady himself. But there was no reply—he already knew the answer.

As Rhys stepped into the clearing on the Grim hill, he saw huge dark storm clouds massed above the lone tree. A cold wind began to howl through the trees on the edge of the clearing. The rushing sound of an approaching downpour sent him under the tree for cover. The tree shivered and, for a moment, hail rattled to the ground all around him. He stared in disbelief, having never seen hail before.

*Ice coming from the sky before the harvest? Could the world be coming to an end?* Rhys looked up into the dark clouds, thinking he might see the Christ Himself and His angels coming to visit His kingdom on earth. Alayn had told him that was how the world would end. He heard it from a boy whose uncle was a monk.

After a few minutes, the hail stopped and the dark clouds passed, except for a single black patch to the south. Rhys grabbed the lowest limb of the tree and began to climb. When he reached the top of the tree, his heart began to pound. He could see the steeple of the abbey chapel, but only barely amidst a cloud of black smoke. The abbey was on fire.

\* \* \*

The three of us sat on the edge of the clearing near the cottage while a bee droned diligently in search of clover. We tried to remain vigilant, but, like the abbey, the cottage's peaceful setting had a lulling effect.

"What do you think?" I asked. "Can devils be redeemed?"

Haelstrum made a humming noise nearly the same pitch as the bee's droning; the befuddled bee suddenly changed direction and found the flower it had been unable to locate. Haelstrum smiled for a second before turning his attention to my question.

"Mankind is made for redemption, angels are not."

"But," I said, "redemption is solely from God. A man or woman neither seeks it nor earns it apart from Him."

"Yes, but mankind is made incomplete. He is born totally dependent on his father and mother. It is only through years of training and growing that he learns to take care of himself and others. We, on the other hand, are able to think and work from the moment we're created."

I told Haelstrum that I did not see what that had to do with redemption.

Haelstrum replied, "The process of redemption for man begins when he sees, through the help of the Spirit, that he is, and always will be, incomplete. That is when he begins to seek reconciliation with his heavenly Father—and becomes willingly dependent again. The process is unique to the nature of mankind—angels, for better or worse, are complete. We are not haunted by a broken relationship to a father as they are."

"I've heard rumors of angels turning back from evil." Zophar said.

Haelstrum didn't respond. Instead, he turned his head to one side and seemed to be listening to something far away.

"I've heard the rumors as well, Zophar," I said. "But I've never found anyone who could say they had found them to be true."

Haelstrum held a finger to his lips. Zophar and I waited, listening. Suddenly Haelstrum stood and looked to the south. We stood and followed his gaze. There, in the southern sky, I saw a massive storm cloud. It had great billows of dark clouds piled up to the top of the sky. In the midst of it, we saw the angel Nuriel, Bringer of Storms. Nuriel was building the storm in the south and slowly moving it north across the sky. What Haelstrum had heard was the wind. It began as a low whine in the distance, caused by gusts shrieking through the tree branches. The sound grew louder as the storm approached. I have seen countless storms on the earth; there was the storm that caused Jonah to be thrown overboard and swallowed by the fish, there was the storm that Elijah prophesied from Mount Carmel, there was even the storm that Jesus rebuked on the sea of Galilee. But this was the first storm I have ever seen brought by Nuriel himself. Nuriel was the size of a mountain. His arms were as massive as the greatest of tree trunks. His great white beard and long white hair whipped back over his shoulders. He churned his arms causing the clouds to roll over and over. He was nearly overhead when pieces of ice began to fall all around us. Nuriel continued stirring the clouds so furiously that, though staring earthward, he did not see us.

I watched in awe as Nuriel and the storm passed. The power and beauty of the storm was nearly like standing before the throne of God—one is caught between competing urges; to flee or to fall on one's face in worship. As the storm passed, Haelstrum knelt and whispered, "Precious be the death of Your saints, O Holy One."

I asked, "What is it, Haelstrum? What has happened?"

"I saw them in the cloud," Haelstrum said in a low voice, looking up. "His saints who were slain; they were in the cloud. Nuriel gathered them from the earth."

I knelt beside Haelstrum and repeated the prayer.

"Iothiel," Zophar said, "Nuriel and the storm passed over the abbey."

I opened my eyes. Zophar was pulling his sword from its scabbard. It came to me, suddenly, what Zophar meant: The spirits of the dead that Nuriel had gathered came from the abbey. What we had feared had come. The abbey was under attack.

I sprang to my feet. "On guard for devils and Dragon! Zophar, where is your charge?"

But Zophar did not hear. He was sprinting across the meadow toward the Grim hill.

Haelstrum and I gripped our swords and searched the forest for signs of approaching devils. I saw no devils, so I sheathed my sword and tucked my robe into my sword belt. "I fear Dragon is in Iconium; Haelstrum, so to Iconium I go."

* * *

Before Carlyle reached the cottage, a wind howled across the meadow from the south. It nearly knocked him over. He found the door open and the cottage in disarray. Chairs were blown over, ink bottles tipped, and parchments scattered about the room. Carlyle leaned his full weight against the door, forcing it closed against the howling wind. He latched the door and drew a deep breath. Slowly he gazed about the wind-ravaged room and heard the words, "Behold, your life." And he knew that, like the room before him, his life was about to change in ways he could not control. Everything familiar to him would soon be whirled about by the wind of God.

Carlyle began to move slowly about the room, picking up parchment and righting bottles of ink. A rapping sound came from outside the cottage. Through a crack in the shutters, he could see hail falling. He wondered where Rhys was. He realized this all had something to do with the young man. He had initially thought of Rhys' presence as a distraction. Now he knew Rhys had been brought by the hand of God, and the things which had been important no longer were. Carlyle knew he must make a choice. He could participate willingly, or he could resist the changes and attempt to keep his life the same. He had made the choice before, many times. It always cost him to say "aye." Even a monk of his age enjoyed some comforts—a few moments of fellowship, a warm meal, a comfortable place to sleep. But to say "nay" was to lose much more. To say "nay" was to lose the voice of the Spirit, for the Spirit only spoke to willing hearts. And to lose the voice of the Spirit was to lose his very own soul.

Carlyle heard footsteps, and Rhys opened the cottage door. He was out of breath from running. His face was pale and his eyes were dark with fear when they met Carlyle's.

"A great column...of black smoke...comes...from the south...from the abbey!"

Carlyle's breath stopped. "Smoke from the abbey?"

Rhys nodded.

Carlyle went to the cottage door and stepped outside. There, above the treetops, he could see thick black smoke spreading across the southern sky. Carlyle turned and faced Rhys. There was a change in the monk's face—his jaw was set, and his eyes had a look of iron. "We leave for the abbey at once," he said in a low voice before returning to the cottage.

Rhys wondered if this was what Carlyle had made him climb the tree for every day. He glanced back at the smoke rising in the sky and thought, *By this time tomorrow we will know what caused that smoke.* Inside the cottage, he found that Carlyle had stripped off the black monk's robe and was pulling on leggings under a tunic. It was the dress of a common man, not a monk. Rhys stared at him. Carlyle met his gaze and said, "Sometimes the path we follow leads in ways that are hard to explain. Besides, the monk's robe is not suited to running through the forest."

Carlyle folded the robe and placed food in it, rolling it up like a pouch and tying it to his waist.

Rhys stood in bewildered silence till the older man commanded him, "Put the leather wrap with the sword and bow shaft on your back. The loop goes around your neck, and the strap you tie around your waist."

"What about your manuscript?" Rhys asked.

"I'll not be working on it for a while."

Rhys strapped the sword and bow sling to his back as

Carlyle had told him.

"Do you think the abbey has been attacked by raiders from the north?" Rhys asked.

"Raiders often choose abbeys since they rarely put up a fight." Carlyle blew out a lone-burning candle. "I fear the fire that makes that column of smoke, will soon burn our very hearts."

# Chapter 12

## THE DRAGON'S WRATH

"We must reach the abbey by dark," Carlyle told Rhys. "We'll run as far as we can. Then we'll walk till we have the strength to run again."

Rhys nodded and followed as Carlyle began running across the meadow, the robe-pouch bouncing up and down from his belt. They ran toward the Grim hill till Carlyle veered to the right, avoiding the hill and taking a shorter route to the abbey. Their pace slowed to a steady trot. Sweat dripped from Carlyle's face, though he showed no sign of stopping till early afternoon when they came upon a stream. Carlyle drank from the stream, before laying on the ground and closing his eyes. Were it not for the rise and fall of his chest, he would have appeared lifeless.

After his drink, Rhys removed the leather wrap and laid it on the ground next to where he stretched out to rest. "I thought monks had no use for such weapons," he said.

Carlyle opened his eyes and stared up at the clouds. "That has not always been so. I began my service at the abbey of Lindisfarne. They told stories of brothers of old in Hibernia who fought when justice demanded it."

"I can't imagine Father Wilfrid or the brothers of the abbey taking up arms."

"Not Father Wilfrid," Carlyle agreed. "Abbeys are still places of meditation and prayer. But the warriors are gone."

Rhys tried to imagine the monks of Iconium fighting Acwellen's thanes. "Why do they not fight?"

Carlyle stood up slowly, wiping the sweat from his face. "Because monks are better at fighting the enemy when he attacks from within than when he attacks through others."

"Enemy? You mean the Devil?"

Carlyle began wading across the stream. "Devils know they cannot attack the Creator," he said, "so they attack His weakest and most precious creature. It matters little to them whether they attack through evil thoughts or the priest of Grim or raiders from the north sea."

Rhys glanced about and lowered his voice as he stepped into the water after Carlyle, "The carpenter's son said his father saw the devil once. He had the horns of a goat and the tail of a donkey. Have you seen him?"

"Nay. But I've seen his evil deeds."

"Why would he want to hurt the likes of us?" Rhys asked, climbing the stream bed to where Carlyle stood. "I've never done anything to bother him."

"You bear the image of God, do you not?" demanded Carlyle.

Rhys had never thought about being in the image of God. There was no priest or church in Edenton, but everyone believed in Christ and the virgin Mary. They believed, even more, in the Devil; perhaps because he reminded them of Grim. And, as it was, they had many odd practices that Rhys had been told were supposed to keep the Devil away.

Rhys quickened his steps to keep pace with Carlyle. He thought about his life—working in the smith shop, hunting and fighting with Alayn, Mother's kindness and Ormod's anger—he had never thought of it as a war between good and evil. It was just life; the way it was for everyone in the village. But now, with Alayn arrested and himself living in the forest like a hunted animal, he wondered, *Could it be that life is a battle against evil, against the very Devil himself?*

\* \* \*

I reached the abbey by mid-day and entered quietly through the back gate. For a moment, I could only stand and gaze at the destruction. The chapel roof was no more than a black hole. Flames were swallowing the dorter. The refectory's stones were blackened as fire licked around it. Its thatched roof was gone. The roses in front of the refectory were scorched and wilted. A torn piece of black cloth, caught on a rose bush, flapped in the breeze. The abbey was silent except for the crackling of the hungry flames.

I crossed the courtyard looking for signs of men or of angels. On the walkway near the front gate were several large blood-stains. A trail of smaller stains ran from the walkway to the stable. I started for the stable when I saw an angel, unmoving and faded, lying next to the chapel. *I'll need to get him and any others to Orion*, I thought. Inside the stable, I found two bodies covered head-to-foot with blankets. The third was blanketed to his neck and attended by a stocky monk who bent over him, giving him a drink of water.

"Iothiel."

I spun around to see Mythiel. His once-glowing face was pallid and shrunken in pain. He held his sword loosely at his side.

"Mythiel, you are injured. You must go to Orion!"

Mythiel shook his head weakly. "There are men left here that I must guard until Rathiel and Mycynn return from Orion."

"I'll guard the abbey. Go to Orion."

Mythiel shook his head again. "I'll not go." He sank to his knees, the last of his energy flowing out of him. "Though Dragon burn every stone and timber; though he make this plot of earth as hell itself; I am the guardian of this realm...." Mythiel tried to prop himself up with his sword; but strength abandoned him, and he slumped to the ground.

I bent down and laid a hand on him. "You could not have

withstood Dragon with a few dozen angels, no matter how valiantly they fought. Rest now so you can fight again."

I heard voices in the courtyard and looked over the stable to see Rathiel and Mycynn coming. "There, by the chapel wall you will find a wounded angel," I said, pointing to the spot.

Rathiel walked to the chapel wall and lifted the faint form. I motioned to Mycynn. "Here you will find your captain, Mythiel."

Mycynn leaned over the dim form of Mythiel and removed the sword from his hand. He lifted his captain gently in his arms.

"Will you remain here to guard those who are left at the abbey?" he asked.

I nodded. "Godspeed."

\* \* \*

The light was fading from the forest when Carlyle and Rhys came upon a large rock. Carlyle sat and rested his legs. "The abbey's not much farther," he said, taking bread and onions from a pouch. As they ate in the darkening woods, Carlyle gazed into the trees. "I would not hope to sleep long tonight. Depending on what we find, there may be much yet to do."

Rhys wondered what a village was like after a raid. As boys, he and Alayn fought imaginary raiders from the north. But they always won their pretend battles. And he had never given much thought to what it would be like after the raiders leave a looted and burned village.

When they started again for the abbey, there was just enough light to see the black forms of trees and branches in front of them. Frogs began croaking in a pond somewhere nearby. Rhys noticed that Carlyle had begun favoring his right leg. Suddenly Carlyle stopped. They had come to the road that Rhys had traveled previously with Bors and Elene. Carlyle turned and whispered, "We shall take this road to the village. But be careful to make no noise. If you see anyone, take to the trees without delay. Do you understand?"

Rhys nodded. He was struck by the thought of how odd it was to have to flee and return to such a place of peace under the cover of darkness. Carlyle stayed to the edge of the road, within a few steps of the trees. Rhys followed. Ahead they could see where the road left the forest and entered Iconium. It was less dark beyond the trees. Rhys wondered if the moon had come out or if the sky still held the last rays of twilight.

The abbey walls and the sky above it were lit with the orange glow of fire. They could still see a thin column of black smoke disappearing into the dark blue sky. The thatch roof of the chapel, once visible above the abbey walls, was gone. Carlyle headed for the back gateway in a limping gait that looked as if he were skipping. Rhys followed, afraid of what they might find.

They stopped in the back entrance of the abbey courtyard. Like the chapel, the dorter, the scriptorium, and the refectory no longer had roofs. The walls to each of the buildings were blackened or burned. Where the doors to the buildings had been, there were gaping black holes. They saw no one. Carlyle limped slowly across the courtyard toward the dormitory. Rhys stared at the smoldering ruins in disbelief. From the dormitory, a monk, covered with black soot and carrying a wooden bucket, appeared through the burned-out doorway. The soot-covered man and Carlyle gazed at one another.

"Forgive me, brother," Carlyle said, "But I do not recognize you in this darkness. What is your name?"

"Leof," was the strained reply of the dark-faced man.

"Leof, for the love of Saint Peter, what happened here? Was it raiders from the north sea?"

Leof shook his head wearily. "Acwellen's thanes came looking for a fugitive." Leof lowered his eyes and took a deep breath. "When Father Wilfrid told them he was not here...they...." He began to sob, and his body sagged so that he would have collapsed had Carlyle not caught him. At the mention of the fugitive, Rhys gasped as if he had been punched in the bowels.

Carlyle lowered the sobbing man to the ground. "Leof," he asked quietly, "Where is Father Wilfrid?"

Leof smeared the soot and tears across his cheeks with his sleeve. He took a couple of deep breaths and stood up. Carlyle held his arm to steady him, but Leof raised his hand to signal that he could stand. He led them across the courtyard to the stable. Rhys followed, gazing with horror at the ruins around him.

The stable was lighted by a torch hanging on the wall. Leof and Rhys stood watching just outside as Carlyle entered. A man lying on a straw mat was covered to the chin with a blood-stained woolen blanket. Next to him knelt a stocky young monk named Herlwin, his round face and broad arms smeared with soot. Herlwin looked up at Carlyle and nodded with a grim, tear-streaked gaze. Carlyle knelt down and touched the abbot's hand.

"Father Wilfrid, 'tis Carlyle," he said in a low voice.

The abbot opened his eyes and looked up at Carlyle. His face was pale and drawn. He smiled faintly and asked for a drink of water. Herlwin lifted the injured man's head long enough to give him a drink from a leather pouch. Afterward, Father Wilfrid looked up at Carlyle. In a strained whisper he said, "You were right. The dragon came."

Carlyle shook his head. "No one knew…."

"…I was wrong," the abbot closed his eyes but went on slowly, "…didn't believe you. Forgive me."

"You've always done what you believed was right, Father Wilfrid. There is no need to ask forgiveness for that."

"But they died…like sheep to the slaughter," he whispered. "Coming is He?" The abbot nodded weakly, took a final breath and lay still.

Herlwin began to sob, quietly at first, but then uncontrollably. He rose and left Carlyle alone in the stable. Carlyle wiped a tear from his check as he looked at the man with whom he had so often disagreed. He laid his hand on the abbot's forehead and prayed that he would have a peaceful entrance into heaven. Then he pulled the blanket over Father Wilfred's head and stared at the two other bodies in the stable. He wondered why Acwellen would do such a thing; what fugitive would be so important to him?

Another voice came to him; one he had wrestled with before. This voice asked why God would allow such a thing to happen. Carlyle rose and walked out of the stable into the darkness. He breathed deeply. The moist night air was heavy with smoke from the smoldering fire. A few stars peeked down through the smoke and clouds. Carlyle stared back at them and sighed. *I will not let that voice have my heart again,* he told himself. He looked around and saw Leof, Rhys, and Herlwin sitting beneath a tree on the edge of the courtyard, their dark forms ringed in orange light from the smoldering embers of the fire.

Rhys was staring at the small flames on the side of the refectory when he heard Carlyle approaching. The monk limped to the tree and leaned against it. Leof stared at the ground while Herlwin hid his face in his hands and wept softly.

Carlyle asked Leof where the rest of the brothers were. Leof nodded in the direction of Iconium. He said some had gone into Iconium and were staying with townsfolk. Others had gone to the homes of family or friends in various parts of Wessex.

"You and Herlwin are the only brothers left at the abbey?" Carlyle asked.

Herlwin wiped his face with the back of his hand and looked up at Carlyle. "We are the only brothers left at the abbey who are alive."

"Who else was killed?"

"Petrus and Gildon. Gildon was with Father Wilfrid when he told the reeve that the one they sought was not here. But the reeve and the thanes cut down the two of them. They were unarmed, Brother Carlyle. It was murder as sure as we sit here."

"What about Petrus?"

"Petrus had a sword hidden under his sleeping mat. When

he saw what they did to Father Wilfrid and Gildon, he said not a word, but went to his mat and got the sword." The monk tried to shake the memory from his head. "He would have taken them all on. He was fighting one thane when another caught him from behind. There was nothing we could do." The monk turned away, his breath coming in angry sobs.

# Chapter 13

## GUARDIAN OF THE REALM

The next morning I looked up the road to the cemetery and saw a hooded figure beneath a tree. The creature's face was not visible, except for dark spots where the eyes had once been. It seemed to watch the abbey as it swayed like a willow branch blowing in the wind. Another figure stood near the line of trees south of the road.

To Zophar standing next to me, I said, "Like vultures, drawn by the scent of death."

Zophar groaned in disgust. "Do they fight?"

"This kind attacks the heart of man rather than his body. They seek to twist a man's natural grief into despair, rendering him helpless."

As we watched, another figure appeared on the Edenton road next to the cemetery. "Should we not try to stop them?" Zophar asked.

"The heart is fair game for good or evil."

\* \* \*

Rhys woke with the smell of smoke drifting through his head. He heard a rooster crowing in Iconium and quiet voices nearby. He stretched, sat up, and looked around. Carlyle and

Leof were standing at the burned entrance to the refectory. Rhys had learned enough about monks to know that their routine was to rise early for morning prayers. Herlwin, however, was still curled up under his blanket, mumbling prayers in his sleep.

Rhys pulled on his brogues and went to the monks. Carlyle nodded to him. Leof handed him a wooden cup of warm ale and said dutifully, "Let us be thankful that the Lord has sustained us for another night."

As he took the cup, Rhys pondered being thankful in the midst of burned buildings and the slaughtered men. At least Acwellen's thanes had not come back and killed them all. He was thankful for that. He sipped the ale, letting it warm his body and thinking, *Tell them everything. They should know who you are and why Acwellen's men did what they did.* But he kept quiet, wondering what Bors would say. He glanced around at the burned buildings and recalled Elene's words, "Remember whose son you are." *These buildings are a grim reminder of that*, he thought.

Carlyle sighed, staring at the burned stone walls that had been the scriptorium. "It'll be graves that must be dug today."

Rhys nodded.

Herlwin stirred and sat up, looking like a dog that had been caught in the rain. The hair around his tonsure was matted, streaks of soot smeared his face, and his eyes were puffy from sleep. He pulled on his brogues and stood up, motioning at the cup Rhys held in his hand. "I suppose there is a wee bit of ale left, aye?"

"One cup," Leof said handing the drink to Herlwin. "We thought you might be wanting it."

"Aye," Herlwin said, approving their kindness with a grin. He gulped down the drink and wiped his mouth with the back of his hand. Licking his lips, he peered at the bottom of the cup as if he hoped more ale would appear. Then the smile left his face. He nodded earnestly at the two monks. "I suppose there is work to be done today. Tell me forthwith. What are we to do?"

"Since you are one to speak plainly," Carlyle replied, "the youngest and the strongest dig the graves. I'll see if we can save anything from the fires. Leof is going to see the village carpenter about building the burial boxes."

Herlwin nodded soberly and looked at Rhys. "I see then that you and I will test our strength today. Let us not be found wanting. For Leof and Carlyle here are trusting us to get these graves dug. We shall work as surely as the sun does shine, aye?"

\* \* \*

Mycynn, Herlwin's guardian, returned from Orion. The two of us, along with Zophar, followed Rhys, Herlwin, and Leof to the cemetery. When we neared the cemetery gate, the two willow-like devils moved away quietly. Beneath their hoods, we could see ash-colored faces with dark rings around sunken eyes. Across the road from the cemetery, six more devils stood silently watching.

Zophar moved close to me and whispered, "They bear no arms, Iothiel. Why not strike at them now before more arrive? I've heard of devils that can maim an armed angel with just their nails and teeth."

I shook my head. "Let the ordeal unfold. We must know what is in the hearts of these men."

\* \* \*

Leof marked three spots near the front of the cemetery for the graves. He handed Rhys and Herlwin a spade each. Herlwin said something and began digging. Rhys pushed the spade into the ground and thought back to the day when he and Bors had stopped there on their way to the abbey. He wondered if Bors had dug Erlan's grave, and he recalled Carlyle's comment on monks fighting the enemy within better than when the enemy attacks through others. *A field of battle; is that what this is—a battle against evil? How did I become involved in a battle I didn't even know about?*

Herlwin stopped digging and turned to Rhys. "We shall be digging here for a bit, so I suppose it would not hurt for us to pass the time in conversation. Actually, it would be better. We could converse and work at the same time. Not that it be the way of the Benedictine monk; no, they cherish their silence, I can tell you. But if silence makes you nervous or be not your way, then I say let us use the time to come to know each other. And, to tell you the truth, silence be no great friend of mine. Many, many things I treasure in life at the abbey; however, I must confess, silence be not one of them. Take this very situation, for instance. Here we are working away side-by-side. You do not know me, nor I you. What better way to pass this time digging than in fellowship one with another as the holy writings of our Lord's apostles say. Indeed, this be the very way we encourage one another."

Herlwin put his brogue on the spade and pressed it into the ground. "But maybe you are the kind who prefers silence. I would not presume upon you, my friend. As I think upon it, you do seem like the quiet type. And if that be your way of things, then upon my word we shall work in silence and say no more." Herlwin closed his mouth and held his hand across it, indicating that not another word would issue from it till Rhys agreed.

Rhys stopped digging for a moment and looked at the monk; Herlwin was different than the other monks. Words seemed to spill out of him like water poured over a beaver's dam, while the other monks spent words carefully, as if they were precious coins. Rhys wondered if Herlwin was always like this or whether the talk gotten all pent up from the long periods of silence.

"Nay Herlwin. I prefer the conversation."

Herlwin smiled broadly and loosened another spade of earth. "Well, as I say friend, it will be an encouragement to us both, that I assure you. And I am eager to hear your story."

*With a little luck,* thought Rhys to himself, *this monk will not be quiet long enough for me to have to tell it.*

"But," Herlwin continued, "lest we leave the subject of silence quietly, without telling the whole story, I will say this; it is the one thing that was about to finish my life as a monk. I was ready to leave the abbey. I was at my wit's end. I could not take another day of it."

"Did you tell Father Wilfrid you were considering leaving?" Rhys asked.

"Huhh!" Herlwin laughed, shaking his head. "Every single day I was warned about talking when I was not supposed to! I think Father Wilfrid knew that silence was no great attribute of mine."

"Had you left, where would you have gone?"

The monk smiled at the question. "Aye, a question with substance, my young friend. One cannot leave a place without going somewhere! One cannot just wander off into the woods eating wild berries. One has to have a plan. I suppose I would have gone to the home of my mother and brother. At least, that would do till I had some other hope. Maybe I could go to the house of a lord where I could teach his children their letters. To tell you the truth, I've not given it much thought."

"Your mother and brother," repeated Rhys. "Do they live around here?"

"Northwest. Near the waters of the great sea. They have animals—three pigs and a cow; enough for them to live on, anyway."

Rhys thought of the sea. He had never been to it. But he realized if he were being pursued by Acwellen's thanes, the sea could block his flight, leaving him trapped.

"What is northeast of Iconium?" he asked.

Herlwin wrinkled his nose thoughtfully. "I've always been told that if one goes far enough east and a bit north, he will come to the great city. Whether that be true, I know not."

Rhys and Herlwin worked till early afternoon, when Leof returned from Iconium with a loaf of bread and some cheese. Rhys took his portion of bread and cheese to the back of the cemetery. He sat with his back to a tree, facing the weathered white cross marking Erlan's grave.

Rhys looked at Erlan's cross and imagined a lord, fighting sword-to-sword to the death. *How can I be like him?* Rhys wondered. *I'm no warrior. Maybe if I sit here at Erlan's grave, it will come to me. Maybe, somehow, I will know what it means to be a lord.* So he sat and listened. But he heard nothing except the wind blowing through the trees.

Rhys glanced about and saw that Leof was gone. Herlwin had begun digging again, so Rhys went back to the knee-deep hole he had started and took up his spade. Herlwin nodded to him, waiting for him to speak. Rhys nodded back. "I suppose you are waiting to hear my story," he said as he began digging. He thought of what he should say; how much of the story Bors would want him to tell. "There be little enough to tell" he began, and then he looked up. There at the gate of the cemetery stood a bear of a man in a hooded robe, like the black robes of the abbey's monks, only brown. Herlwin followed Rhys' startled gaze as the man approached them.

"Welcome, friend," Herlwin said. He turned to Rhys. "Have no fear. He appears to be a man of the cross, though a different order."

The stranger was a large, fleshy man with pale skin that gathered under his bearded chin in rolls. His dark eyes appeared dull, as if he saw nothing that pleased him. The monk was in the middle of his days, younger than Carlyle but a little older than Herlwin.

The man nodded toward the abbey ruins. "I saw the smoke," he said in a husky voice. "I assume the fire was set by infidels—raiders from the north?"

"These were no infidels from the north," Herlwin replied. "These were Acwellen's thanes from Edenton. Edenton is southwest, down that very road behind you."

The man's eyes widened. "A lord from the village of Edenton sent his men to destroy the abbey? What, pray tell, would provoke him to do such a thing?"

"They said they were looking for someone. The abbot explained he was not here, but they didn't believe him, murdered the abbot and two brothers." Herlwin turned and motioned toward the burned buildings of the abbey. "As you can well see, they set fire to the abbey."

"Great saints in heaven!" exclaimed the man. "They burned it because they were looking for someone? Must be no common thief! I've seen this kind of destruction by raiders from the north sea, never by a lord of Wessex. Are you sure they weren't raiders?"

Herlwin wrinkled his brow in concern. "Lord Acwellen's thanes. I saw them myself."

The stranger shook his head in disbelief.

"You are not of the Benedictine order," Herlwin said.

"Nay, I've been called by our Lord to gather alms and give them to the poor. Baldric's me name."

Herlwin smiled and nodded at this. "Mine's Herlwin, a brother of the Abbey at Iconium, or what remains of it. And this is Rhys," he said, gesturing to the young man, "A friend of the abbey."

Rhys nodded his greeting to Baldric. Baldric met Rhys' gaze with eyes that lingered such that he made a shiver run down the young man's back.

\* \* \*

Baldric was accompanied by two large devils armed with swords. Mycynn and Zophar reached for their swords hilts. I put my hand on Zophar's shoulder to steady him. The devils glared at us but did not make any moves toward starting a fight.

\* \* \*

As he was friendly by nature, Herlwin took the stranger, Baldric, to the abbey ruins to give him bread and cheese. It was nearly dark when Carlyle and Leof came to the cemetery. By that time, Rhys' back ached and the palms of his hands blistered from hours of handling the spade.

"The graves are deep enough," Carlyle said. "There is porridge in the pot. Come and eat."

Herlwin and Baldric sat near the fire with their backs to stones from the burned walls. At the arrival of Rhys, Carlyle and Leof, Baldric abruptly stopped talking and looked up. Herlwin greeted Rhys with a worried smile. "There you are, Rhys! Back from digging the graves, aye? You've just now been named in our discussion. Baldric here happened to ask me," Herlwin hesitated, a pained look crossed his face, "be you the one that Acwellen's thanes where hunting?"

Rhys looked from Herlwin to the fleshy Baldric. He felt his heart pounding like a hammer in Ormod's shop. Every eye turned on him, waiting for him to speak. A voice inside him warned him not to tell. *Baldric must have seen that Herlwin's tongue was loose*, Rhys thought. *Why else would he have asked Herlwin this question?* But he knew that his silence was as much an answer as anything he might say. "I am," he said, quietly.

Baldric cleared his throat and muttered, "Aye? I suppose 'tis no great matter. Just got me curiosity."

Herlwin, realizing he had said too much, bowed his head to avoid Rhys' gaze. Silence followed like a gaping hole, but Rhys refused to fill it. He burned with anger toward the meddlesome stranger. *If he wants to know more*, Rhys thought, *let him ask.* Baldric, however, did not pursue the subject with Rhys. Instead, he addressed the sheepish Herlwin, "Have you been to the abbey at Exeter? The abbot there tells of a scribe who has created a manuscript of Beowulf and characters from the Lord's book."

Delighted to have a different subject to discuss, Herlwin shook his head vigorously. "Nay, though I have heard tell of it. Tales for the hardy of heart and venturesome of spirit, they say! And I must admit, regretfully, that I have not visited Exeter. But Carlyle has, and he told me of this very manuscript. He's read parts of it, I believe. Is that not true, Carlyle?"

Carlyle eyed Baldric in silence.

Baldric snorted at Herlwin's enthusiasm. "Filled with

112

fantasy, I hear; nothing but vain speculations about heaven, hell, angels, and demons. A man ought not fill his mind with such speculations. It warps the soul like a piece of green wood."

Herlwin fell silent, perplexed that this promising new subject of conversation had soured so quickly. But Carlyle said to Baldric, "The abbot at Exeter, what's his name?"

"Albinus."

"You've spoken with him on your recent travels?"

"I've just come from Exeter, gathering food for the poor." Baldric said the word "poor" as if it were some distasteful creature he had met on his journey.

"You must have been traveling slowly then, for Albinus has been dead these three years," Carlyle replied sharply. "You're no monk, and I daresay you know not the poor. You are a liar; a man of Acwellen's, I don't doubt. You'll find no welcome in our company, for we'll not sup with such a dishonest creature as you!"

Baldric was up on his feet quickly for such a large man. He started at Carlyle, but before he could get past the fire Herlwin stood in his way.

"I'm loose of tongue," Herlwin admitted, his voice breaking with tension. "But I'll be not a coward."

The massive Baldric looked at the faces of the four men before him and saw that everyone opposed him. "The devil take the lot of you!" he cried. He spat on the ground and stalked off into the evening toward Edenton.

\* \* \*

We watched the armed devils follow Baldric up the road to Edenton. Zophar said, "Bless him, that Carlyle has made our job a little easier."

"Beware," Haelstrum replied. "What goes into the night may return unexpected."

\* \* \*

With Baldric gone, the men breathed again, but their hearts remained heavy.

"Please forgive me, brothers," Herlwin lamented. "My tongue is a wild fire, and it has brought the judgment of God upon us."

Carlyle said nothing; though his dark gaze at Herlwin was a rebuke as much as any that was ever spoken. He went to the pot and began dipping porridge. When they each had a bowl, he said, "For this meal, we will suspend the vow of silence." Then, to Rhys he said, "There is something you have kept from us, which we must now hear."

Rhys took a deep breath. The three men waited. "I was hunting deer with a friend on freedman's land. We separated when I was tracking a stag. I heard my friend cry out. Acwellen's thanes caught him; they said he was poaching. But I ran away…"

Rhys paused. They all knew there was more to the story; the abbey was not burned over a matter of poaching. "They may also be looking for me because they believe I was…or be…Lord Erlan's son."

A moment of stunned silence passed before Herlwin gasped, "You mean Lady Elene's father? The one that Acwellen killed and lies buried in the cemetery on yonder hill?"

Rhys nodded.

"Lady Elene has been in Iconium since she was a child," Carlyle said. "How is it that Erlan's son would be hidden all these years?"

"I was raised by a blacksmith named Ormod in Edenton. After Alayn was arrested for poaching, Ormod told me that I was the son of Lord Erlan, although he was drunk when he told me. And Bors told me that Lord Erlan's wife was in childbirth the same day that Lord Erlan was killed, which is the day I was born.

"Bors also swore that I favor Lord Erlan."

Herlwin groaned, "Acwellen's thanes will return and kill us all. If you could only cast me into the sea as the sailors did with

Jonah—I'll swear my tongue has brought this judgment."

"I be the one to cast away," said Rhys. "I be the one who brought this destruction on the abbey."

"If death be our fate, 'tis God's will," Leof reassured them.

Carlyle raised an eyebrow and stared into the fire.

# Chapter 14

## THE BURIAL

The second morning after the burning of the abbey a thick, gray sky covered Iconium so completely that it made one wonder if the sun could be seen from any place on earth. The rain began at dawn, and it drove the men to the shelter of the stable. Herlwin remarked that the clouds had more water than all the sea. And then, even he fell silent and they finished what ale they had. Every so often Rhys glanced nervously at the opposite side of the stable where the three bodies lie wrapped in linen.

As the rain weakened to a light mist, clopping and clattering sounds came from the courtyard. The noise made Rhys jump, but Herlwin said, "Tis the carpenter and his cart."

A man, gray-bearded and wearing a woolen hood, came into view. He was leading an ox that pulled a cart with two large wooden wheels. On the cart, were three long wooden boxes, each the size of a man. The carpenter nodded to the monks who helped him unload the boxes and set them on the floor of the stable.

"Be a wet day for a burial," the carpenter said. He lifted the lid off the first box.

Carlyle motioned to Rhys. "Take the abbot's shoulders, and let us lift him in."

Rhys looked down at the abbot's body. He took a deep breath, reached under the shoulders, and lifted. Carlyle lifted from the knees, and so they placed the body into the box. The carpenter placed the lid back on the box, nailing it closed.

"Now Petrus," Carlyle said.

They lifted Petrus' body into the box, then Gildon's. The carpenter nailed the lid on each box as it was closed. He motioned for the men to each take a corner, and they carried the burial boxes, one by one, to the wooden cart.

"Rain's lessened," the carpenter said, looking up. He took hold of the ox's halter and began to lead it up the road toward the cemetery. The monks and Rhys followed. Leof took a tin whistle from his cloak and began to play a dirge.

\* \* \*

As we followed the funeral procession, we could see half a dozen devils waiting near the cemetery. Murmuring sounds came from them, a sort of grievous muttering in some devilish tongue.

Zophar laid hold of his sword hilt. "I'll give them a taste of despair," he swore.

"Hold fast." I told him. "This moment is not meant to test your sword, Zophar."

\* \* \*

Before they reached the cemetery, Leof stopped playing the tin whistle and wiped his nose with his sleeve. Herlwin wept quietly; Carlyle blinked the mist from his eyes. A voice in the back of Rhys' mind kept saying, *'Tis all your fault* till his shoulders sagged and his head bowed.

The carpenter led the ox to the cemetery gate and stopped. Carlyle stepped next to one of the wooden boxes. "Let's begin with Gildon."

They lifted the box and carried it to a grassy spot next to the grave. With the box on the ground, Rhys and Herlwin lifted the front so the carpenter could put a rope under it. They placed a rope in the back as well so they could lower the burial box into the grave. In this manner, they lowered each of the boxes into the graves. Abbot Wilfrid was placed in the middle grave and Petrus on the right.

"From the earth we were made and to the earth we shall return until the coming of the Lord," Carlyle proclaimed. The brothers nodded and prayed silently. Then Herlwin and Leof shoveled a little mud over the burial boxes.

"You'll want to finish that once the mud dries," muttered the carpenter, turning back to his cart. "I'll be going to dry me ox." He took the ox's halter and began leading it back to Iconium.

\* \* \*

The murmuring of the devils increased as they swayed in the wind and the mist. I could not understand their tongue, but the sound they made brought to mind deaths that I had witnessed—a child weakened by illness, a farmer in the field at the hand of his jealous neighbor, raids, battles, executions.

\* \* \*

At the head of each grave, Carlyle placed a white stone and a small wooden cross with a name carved on it. They sang a hymn, their voices thick with emotion. Leof prayed a short prayer for the departed.

Herlwin wiped his face with his sleeve and said, "They're in a far better place now, aren't they?"

Carlyle and Leof nodded.

"We should be glad for them," Leof said softly. But each man struggled with a greater darkness of heart than they had known since the destruction of the abbey.

\* \* \*

The devils crossed the road and moved toward the cemetery. We stepped next to our charges and waited with our hands on our sword hilts. Muttering still, the devils slowly, deliberately approached the men.

\* \* \*

Overwhelmed by grief, the men struggled to hold fast to what they believed about death—that there was such a place as heaven and that the men they buried would be resurrected into the afterlife. Rhys sank to his knees before Abbot Wilfrid's grave. Gazing at the burial box, he felt the shadow of death robbing him of breath and churning his bowels. Herlwin sobbed quietly, and Leof covered his face with his hands.

\* \* \*

As we watched, the devils moved in groups of two or three toward each man. The devils reached out dark, gnarled hands; their fingertips mere inches from the heads of the unsuspecting men. I glanced at Zophar and his eyes met mine. We held steady, waiting to draw our swords at the first movement a devil made to cause bodily harm to our charges.

\* \* \*

But then, among the mourning men, staggered by grief, the story of Beowulf came to Carlyle's mind. He looked at Rhys, and anger began to rise in him. The grief he saw was more than any natural sadness. It was crippling. And the words Beowulf spoke to old King Hrothgar came back to Carlyle like a flood.

"On to your feet, guardian of the realm!"

The words of Beowulf, spoken by Carlyle, penetrated the fog that shrouded Rhys' heart and mind. He wiped the rain from his face and looked up at Carlyle.

"Was your father not the murdered lord of Edenton?" Carlyle demanded. "Are you not his son and his heir?"

"Aye."

"Then you are the guardian of Edenton and all its subjects. Heed Beowulf's words to King Hrothgar as the King wept over his murdered advisor, 'Do not, as a man of reason, give yourself up to grief. 'Tis a finer thing in any man that he should avenge his friend than that he should unduly mourn. Each one of us must live in expectation of an end of life in this world: let him who can gain good repute before death—that is the finest thing thereafter for the lifeless man.'"

Rhys blinked glassy eyes. He didn't know what Carlyle meant or intended, but he wiped his sleeve across his face and got to his feet.

"I beg you, Brother Carlyle, what shall I do? Should I go to Edenton? Attack Acwellen's thanes barehanded?"

"Better that than draining your life out in tears for the abbot. No one will tell that story around the evening fire."

\* \* \*

The devils hands hovered over the men's heads as if despair dripped from the spirits' fingers into the weakened minds of the men. But for the moment, their murmuring and muttering lessened as they waited to see what the effect of Carlyle's words would be.

\* \* \*

Red-eyed Herlwin stood. "The bard's words have never been more true, Brother Carlyle. If you have another sword, I will take it up with you. Ah, but I can use Petrus' sword, may he rest in peace."

"But is not vengeance the Lord's work alone?" Leof asked.

"Aye," Carlyle replied, "if you mean to simply repay an evil act. But He may well call us to set things right—to protect the innocent and rescue the oppressed."

\* \* \*

The devils' spell of despair seemed to have broken. Gnarled hands withdrew from the men. One of the devils whirled around and glared at Carlyle.

"Cursed little man," the devil sputtered. He took a step toward Carlyle and grabbed for his throat. But Haelstrum seized the devil's wrist with one hand and held his sword to the devil's chest with the other. Their eyes met briefly, before the devil screamed and wrenched itself from the angel's grasp. He fell back, picked himself up, and ran wailing into the cover of the trees.

Several devils turned and ran after the fleeing spirit. The rest of them backed to the cemetery road, glaring at Carlyle and Haelstrum and chattering to themselves.

We rejoiced in the Creator's goodness: for it was He who had spoken to Carlyle and had prepared him to shepherd the young man's heart. The devils were turned back, not by the sword, but by faith and courage—the very weapons that would be needed to defeat Dragon.

"Edenton may see its true lord yet," Zophar said.

\* \* \*

Carlyle began walking back toward the abbey ruins. Rhys and the two others hurried after him.

"But what are we to do?" Rhys asked.

"As far as we know," Carlyle said without breaking stride, "Baldric is at this very moment telling Acwellen all about what he saw and heard here."

"Then we must leave!" Rhys exclaimed.

"Aye."

"I'll not leave," Leof stated flatly.

The men stopped and turned to look at Leof. He faced Carlyle with grim determination, "Someone must finish filling in the graves as the earth dries. I've no desire to go anywhere else."

"If Baldric be Acwellen's man," Carlyle said, "a day or two from now the reeve and Acwellen's thanes will come riding down this road in search of Rhys."

"Fear has no place in my heart, Brother Carlyle. I will gladly trade this body for heaven's crown whether tomorrow or twenty years from now. I've attended to Father Wilfrid's needs in life, I'll not abandon him now in his death."

"Stand by him as always, Brother Leof!" Herlwin cried. "I should stay as well, though in death the Holy Father might grow as weary of my voice as in life. What says you, Brother Carlyle?"

"Stay if you must, Leof. I would not tell you to do otherwise. We'll leave before the morning light without a hint of where we are going, lest you be questioned. It'll be no lie for you to say you know not where we have gone."

Rhys looked from Carlyle to Leof. "Can't you get someone from the village, like the carpenter, to come fill in the graves? Why take the risk, Brother Leof?"

"Anyone near the cemetery or abbey will be at risk. I would not ask another to take a risk that is mine."

"Then I should stay," Rhys protested. "The brothers' deaths be my fault, after all."

"Oh, you'll be at risk where ever you are," Carlyle replied. "If Acwellen didn't know who you were before, Baldric will make sure he does now. And 'tis you who can hurt Acwellen more than any other. We'll not leave you here like a goose for the fox."

The men gathered round the porridge pot and ate the last of the porridge, gazing at their bowls in silence. So they sat till a flutter of feathers broke the spell as Leof's bird landed on his shoulder.

"Aye! 'Tis an omen!" Herlwin cried. "Hermes who fled the fires has returned!"

Leof touched the bird's crown and spoke softly to him, yet all the men found their hearts felt lighter, like the way one feels when the sun comes out after days of dreary clouds and rain.

The clouds parted a little, and sunlight came back to the abbey courtyard. So with smiles they raised their bowls to Hermes and all the birds and beasts on God's green earth. And Carlyle reminded them how God looked at His creation and said that it was good.

That afternoon, Carlyle was picking through the smoldering dorter ruins when he came to the area where Abbot Wilfred had slept. Under the ashes he found several layers of folded cloth. Carlyle picked up the top layer, wiped off a coating of gray ash, and found that it was a brown monk's habit like the one Baldric had been wearing. *How odd*, Carlyle thought. As far as he knew, Abbot Wilfrid had always been a Benedictine monk, which meant he wore a black habit. He placed it over his shoulder and picked up two more habits. Both were brown, but the last one was much larger than the first two. *Maybe they came from another abbey and Father Wilfrid planned on dying them black*, Carlyle thought. Then, as he held up the large brown habit, an idea came to him—an idea that was so risky and unbelievable that he knew it could not have been his own.

Carlyle found Rhys in the stable carefully cutting a notch in the end of his bow so he could string it. The monk hung the habits over a small timber that braced the roof. "Will you not help salvage what we can from the abbey ruins?" he asked.

Rhys looked up. "The bow must be finished. We'll be needing it for hunting as we hide in the forest."

"Leave it here."

Rhys looked at Carlyle as if he had sprouted another head. "Leave it here? I can hunt deer and hare with it. It be not heavy—I'll carry it myself. It might get stolen or burned if I leave it here."

Carlyle glanced about to make sure they were alone. "We'll not tell Herlwin this till we leave, lest he spill it to Leof," he said quietly before fixing his gaze on Rhys. "Now are you not the true lord of Edenton? And be it not your duty to perform noble deeds and gain good repute?"

Rhys stared at Carlyle, waiting for him to go on.

"Is not this friend of yours, Alayn, worthy of your help?"

"What should we do?"

"Dress in these brown robes and go to Edenton as almonders—monks gathering food for the poor."

Rhys gasped. "Go to Edenton? Where Acwellen himself be...where people know me by name...where Acwellen's thanes be? Why bother walking all the way to Edenton when they may well be here in a day or two looking for me?"

Carlyle sat on a three-legged stool and leaned his back against the wall. "Good questions. But consider these—if you want to help Alayn, where but Edenton could you go? Where would Acwellen least expect you to be? If the reeve and his thanes are coming here in the next couple of days, when would be a better time to go to Edenton?"

Rhys tried to go over each of Carlyle's questions in his mind. It was likely a matter of life and death. He couldn't help thinking it was all foolishness—him being lord of Edenton or lord of anything. The only reasonable thing to do was to go to the sea and hire a boat to take them to Hibernia. He said, "Edenton has been Acwellen's for a long time, and the reeve and his thanes will make sure it stays that way."

Carlyle raised an eyebrow, "Don't you think it's your duty to help your friend?"

"Getting killed will be no help to him!"

"Do you think Lord Erlan would run away?" Carlyle asked.

* * *

I stood watch over the Edenton road when I noticed Haelstrum, Zophar, and Mycynn approaching from the direction of the stable. They came with some news; I could tell from the brisk way they walked.

Haelstrum said, "We just heard Carlyle tell Rhys that he is planning for them to leave for Edenton in the morning."

"Edenton?" I asked. "Are you sure he said Edenton?"

"Carlyle said they would dress in brown monks' robes just as Baldric did," Haelstrum replied.

Zophar added, "They are going to attempt to rescue Alayn."

I didn't know what to say. With Carlyle's influence, Rhys' preparation had begun—but to take on Dragon now?

"What do you think of this plan, Haelstrum?" I asked.

"Carlyle's not one for foolish schemes."

Zophar shook his head and said what we were all thinking, "Dragon and these devils are much too powerful for the four of us. You'll send a message to Gabriel to ask for help, I assume."

"Of course," I told Zophar. I wondered aloud if Bittenrood would be there.

"You know this devil?" Mycynn asked.

I nodded. "His name was Zorran before the fall. We fought the night I first entered Edenton to meet Zophar. Since then I've wondered if he would return to this area upon his release from hell."

"He was one of those who burned the abbey. I heard a devil call his name." Mycynn paused and looked at me. "I'm sorry," he said.

# Chapter 15

## TO EDENTON

The day's shadows would have grown long had the clouds not returned to Iconium and brought more rain. Farmers and children went back inside their cottages to stay dry. But I, appearing as a monk, walked quietly along the muddy road, bent low with my hood over my head. I walked past the village's small brown cottages and ripening gardens. As monks were common in Iconium, no one noticed. On the opposite side of Iconium from the abbey, nearly a quarter of a mile past the village, a path led from the road up a small hill. The path was bordered on each side by several rows of low hanging grapevines. I went to the front door and knocked loudly.

"Who is it?" a husky voice called from inside.

"One who seeks a messenger."

"You've come to the wrong place. A winemaker I be."

"We all toil in the Master's vineyard," I replied.

The door creaked and opened a crack. A dark eye peered from near the top of the door. "What is your name?"

"My name is Iothiel. I need to speak with you, Sargon."

The door opened slowly to show a large, stooping angel with dark, shining eyes, a beak-like nose and white hair that hung to his shoulders. His face reminded me of a hawk, even before I saw the large wings that lay against his back.

"Come in," he said. Sargon glanced about the vineyard before closing the door and standing straight. "Pardon my watchful ways, but devils are thicker than flies on sheep dung these days."

The cottage was small for an angel, but tidy. Next to the fire pit stood a round, three-legged table surrounded by three tall stools. Sargon pulled a stool out for me and took one for himself on the other side of the table.

"Sit," he said. "And let us have a word."

I pulled off the monk's robe which had begun growing tight since I entered the cottage. The two of us in our angelic robes sat facing each other across the table.

"I and three other angels are on a mission to Edenton, but there is a dragon there who is very strong. It will be dangerous. We need to send a message to inform Gabriel of this turn of events."

"I know Dragon, for he is strong," Sargon replied. "He makes my travels difficult. Black-winged devils fill the skies over Edenton. I'll take your message to Gabriel, but I cannot say how long it will take me to get through."

"I ask nothing more. I came disguised so that I might draw as little attention as possible."

"Oh, the evil ones know that I am here, posing as a man," explained Sargon. "But they tend to forget about those who live quietly. And that makes it much easier for me to move between the earth and the heavens. Now, tell me your message, since time is wanting."

"The message is this: four angels and three men are leaving for Edenton tomorrow. The men are Rhys, Carlyle, and Herlwin; he'll know who the angels are. The men are going at Carlyle's counsel. Tell Gabriel we believe this mission is of the Spirit. At Edenton we will face at least a hundred devils, including Dragon, and Acwellen's thanes. If Gabriel has any orders, we need to know immediately. We do not plan to engage them in battle if it can be avoided. But if we are engaged in battle, *we will need help.*" I looked the angel in the eye and said, "Sargon, you must stress this point to him: *We will need help soon* if we are to do battle in Edenton."

Sargon raised his eyebrows. "Given your odds, I think Gabriel will understand your concern. You are confident that Carlyle hears the Whispering Voice?

I nodded.

"And you will be in Edenton two days from today?"

"They are preparing to leave now," I replied. "The journey takes two days, if all goes well. Do you have the message?"

Sargon repeated the message, word for word. Then, he said, "I will go with all haste. But before I do, you must leave quietly, and I will let the devils' attention turn back to their own evil deeds."

I stood. "Go with Godspeed."

* * *

Before sunrise the brothers and Rhys met in the stable. "Give us a quarter of an hour to get out of view before you leave the stable," Carlyle told Leof. "Keep an eye out for the reeve's thanes and, if you can, hide in the woods when they come."

Leof nodded.

Herlwin grabbed Leof's neck with a sob and gave him a bear hug.

"Peace be with you," Leof said quietly.

"Few words are best, brother Leof," Herlwin sniffed. "And you spend them well."

Leof smiled.

"Goodbye," Rhys said.

Carlyle said, "God be with you, Brother Leof."

Carlyle took a pack, handed one to Rhys and one to Herlwin. He led them up the road toward Edenton. As they walked by the cemetery, Rhys looked at the small white cross in the back row of grave markers. Carlyle noticed Rhys gazing toward Erlan's grave. "Rhys, do you believe that you are Lord Erlan's son?" he asked.

Rhys nodded. He sensed Carlyle measuring him; like

Ormod sizing up a piece of iron before pounding it into a sword.

"Then your life must be governed by who you are," Carlyle said, "not by fear of pain or discomfort."

Rhys could feel the weight of it settle on him—just as when Elene told him to remember who his father was. He took a deep breath and looked toward the road to Edenton.

They took the same path through the woods that Rhys had traveled with Bors. Only this time they were leaving Iconium. Herlwin wiped his eyes and glanced back at the road they were leaving.

"Brother Carlyle," he said, "do you think it would do any good if I went back and begged Leof to come with us?"

"Let him be. He's made his choice."

"I suppose we would not want him to know where we be headed." Herlwin studied the path with wrinkled brow. "As far as that be concerned, where are we headed?"

"Edenton."

Herlwin stopped suddenly, his forehead wrinkling the more. "Edenton? Did you say Edenton?"

"Aye," Carlyle said, stopping to look back at the wide-eyed monk. "Rhys is the Lord Guardian of Edenton, and there are wrongs being done there. It'll be his duty to set things right."

Herlwin looked from Carlyle to Rhys. "Would this not be foolish? Be you playing the jester—making crazy while speaking riddles?"

Carlyle turned again and started walking without a word. Rhys shrugged.

"We'll just walk up to Acwellen's manor house and tell him what to do?" Herlwin asked.

"We'll dress in brown robes," Carlyle said over his shoulder, "and go to Edenton as almonders."

"The same game that Baldric played?"

"Aye. And it may have worked if he'd not been a witless rogue."

Herlwin looked wide-eyed at Rhys. Rhys shrugged again as

if to say it made little sense to him, but he knew no better plan.

They reached the cave that evening, weary and hungry. Herlwin had stopped talking; he used the last of his strength to gather firewood. Carlyle had begun to limp again. He laid his pack at the mouth of the cave and lowered himself stiffly to the ground.

Rhys sat next to Carlyle. "You asked me this morning if I believed I was the son of Lord Erlan. You said I was his heir and the guardian and lord of Edenton."

"Aye."

"But I don't know what a lord does! I suppose they do whatever they like; they eat meat and fine breads every day, most likely. They probably go hunting whenever they wish. They make decrees and punish those who don't obey them. And they have servants who wait upon them. But," Rhys said, "I don't even have a home or means. I be raised by a smith, have little learning, and the lord's thanes want to kill me! So just how do I act as a Lord Guardian of Edenton?"

"Ruling often leads to hardships."

"Methinks it doesn't lead to being hunted by thanes," Rhys said hotly.

"The Heaven King was born in a stable. He had no home. His parents had to flee from the murderous King Herod, and He was hung on a cross. Why should your road be any easier?"

Rhys leaned back on his elbows and took a deep breath. He wondered if the life of a commoner might be preferable to the life of a lord after all. And he wondered at the thought that the Lord of All was forced to flee for His life as well.

Carlyle looked toward the sky and rubbed the back of his neck. "It'll be dark soon. We should break bread and look to our prayers."

* * *

Haelstrum told us that no good would come from Dragon knowing of our advance. So, as far as possible, we stayed hidden among the trees as we traveled. We kept our swords ready and our voices low.

That evening I sat by myself a short distance from camp, guarding the road to Edenton. The night was unnaturally silent; none of the typical night noises from crickets or frogs or owls. It troubled me—there were devils near. I stood and slowly drew my sword. The sound of footfalls came from the road. I slipped quietly through the trees to see who it was.

When I reached the road, I stayed back in the trees out of sight. The sound of footfalls grew louder. If it were devils coming, there must be a dozen or more by the sound of them. Suddenly they appeared around a bend in the road. The one in front looked strong, with a broad chest and shoulders. Like a bull, the devil had small horns protruding from his forehead. A sword hung from his side, and a shield was strapped to his arm.

Just as they neared me, the devil raised his hand and the devils stopped. I held my breath, fearing they might see me. He glanced around, as if looking for something.

"Here," came a voice from the wood. For a moment I could not see who had spoken. But then I saw a large snake hanging from a tree branch that stretched out over the road.

The devil said, "We come from hell, searching for Edenton."

"This..." the snake turned its head to look at the road toward Edenton, "this is the way to Edenton."

"Be a dragon there?"

"Dragon rules for seventeen years in Edenton. He is of such strength that the Enemy threatens him not." The snake stared unblinking at the devil. "Why do you go to Edenton?"

"You say the Enemy does not threaten, but Dragon says the Enemy stirs. He calls us forth to fight for him."

The snake stared at the devil. "But Dragon is strong, and Edenton be such a small village."

"And you think the Enemy is weak?" the devil replied. "Maybe you would want to fight Him yourself?"

The devil and the snake gazed at each other silently before

the snake said, "Edenton be a half day's walk up this road...for those who have legs."

The devil turned to those behind him and motioned for them to follow as he started off for Edenton. They were various shapes and sizes. Several were bird-like creatures—beaks for noses and long skinny legs. Some had hairy heads of goats with small horns and hooves for feet. There were bull-headed devils and some that looked like angels but with sunken, lifeless eyes. All carried weapons, whether swords, spears, or bows.

As the devils marched away, I sensed a cold presence behind me. Turning, I saw an ashen face staring at me through the fading evening light.

"I see you spying on our company," hissed the devil. "So with whom do you share these secrets?"

He must have been scouting the road to Edenton for the devil company that just passed. I gazed silently at him. If we were going to fight, I wanted the devils to get as far away as possible before it started.

"I just happened to hear your devil company walking along the road. I was curious."

He had no patience for talk. He raised his sword. I leaped forward and swung my sword at him. The blade missed as the devil fell backward.

I moved between the devil and the road to Edenton. He came back at me, swinging his sword at my head. When I blocked the blow, he turned and ran up the road toward Iconium.

I hoped he would stay on the road where I could see him. But he turned off the road and into the forest. When I reached the trees where he disappeared, I saw a slight opening and dashed through it. A moment later I came out of a stand of fir trees and found myself on the shore of a small, moon-lit lake.

I searched the shores to the left, but saw no sign of life. Suddenly, to my right I heard something crash into the wood. I turned and saw a deer disappear into the trees. And there in the shadows of a beech tree were the dark eyes and watery face of the devil staring at me. His chest rose and fell, panting the way devils do when they are angry.

"What do you want?" the devil hissed.

"To deliver us from evil."

The devil tried to run but slipped. I came on him with such force that he fell back. I made sure that he did not recover.

\* \* \*

After morning prayers, Carlyle, Rhys, and Herlwin dressed in the brown robes. Rhys touched the bare spot on the top of his head, the monk's tonsure, which Carlyle had shaved the previous night. He wondered if the robe and tonsure would be enough to fool those in Edenton who knew him. Meanwhile, Herlwin chattered on about how he had never been to Edenton and how he loved to travel the road and see what is there to be seen. Finally Carlyle silenced him with a cold stare. "Mark it well, Herlwin," he said, "if we gain entrance to Edenton, our lives shall depend on what we say and do. You'll guard your tongue if you do not wish us all killed. Go no further if you cannot commit to that."

Herlwin's smile faded, and he said softly, "You may think my name was Herlwin Be Still. But I was made for fellowship. This adventure that lies before us be borne of fellowship and, more than anything, I would be part of it."

Herlwin bowed slightly to the older monk. "Carlyle, you'll be amazed at the discipline my tongue will know."

"The matter is settled then," Carlyle replied, "as long as you see to it."

They were less than a mile from Edenton when the path joined the Iconium road.

"How much farther to Edenton?" Herlwin asked.

"A couple of bends in the road," Rhys said. "Then it straightens out and you'll see the cottages."

Rhys asked the question he had pondered since they left Iconium. "Carlyle, when we get to Edenton, what shall we do?"

Carlyle raised his left eyebrow thoughtfully. "What should the Lord Guardian of Edenton do?"

Rhys was silent. He had no idea how to answer Carlyle's question.

"You said you had a friend, the smith's son, who was captured by Acwellen's thanes."

Rhys nodded.

"Where is he?"

"Acwellen's keep, most likely."

"He would be one of your subjects, wouldn't he, since you are the Lord Guardian of Edenton?

"I suppose so," Rhys agreed hesitantly. *More like a tease and one to knock wooden swords with*, Rhys thought. It was odd to consider Alayn a subject.

"Then, as guardian, you should come to your subject's aid."

"Be a guardian a fool?" Rhys asked. "Please forgive me for speaking so plainly, but Acwellen is not trusting like you brothers. You believe God will protect you. Acwellen protects himself."

Carlyle stopped and sighed. "Do you think this is all by chance—our meeting, what happened at the abbey? Do you think no one is directing this play?" The dark look in his eyes softened. "If our Lord could go to Jerusalem and bear His cross, then why should we be afraid of going to Edenton?"

Rhys did not reply. Carlyle turned and limped slowly up the road. Herlwin, following behind, said, "Now that we are near the village, where my tongue shall remain as silent as a sunset, should we not have a few words about what we shall find when we get there? Not that I...." The men stopped in the middle of the road and stood listening. Around the bend they could hear the pounding of horses' hooves. Riders were coming toward them. And only a lord or a reeve traveled the roads with men on horses.

Rhys looked around and recognized the trees to the left of them. "Quick!" he said. "Follow me!"

# Chapter 16

## IN THE PRESENCE OF THE ENEMY

Rhys crawled under a thick tangle of brush growing between the trees. Herlwin followed, huffing and puffing as he pulled his large body along the ground.

"Hurry!" Rhys whispered.

Carlyle crawled under the brush last. Lying flat, Rhys peered out as the riders galloped by. "The reeve and four of Acwellen's thanes," he said.

Herlwin looked desperately at Carlyle. "God have mercy! They are headed for Leof in Iconium!"

"Leof's in God's hands," Carlyle said, "just as we are."

Herlwin sighed. They sat silently for a time, praying that Leof would be protected. Then Rhys showed them to a stream where they drank and washed their faces.

"This was our hiding place," Rhys said of the small clearing with a few trees in the center.

Herlwin stretched out on the grass. "'Tis a place where boys dream dreams."

Carlyle sat down and leaned against a tree. "Rhys, when we go to the manor house you must act in a way so as not to draw attention to yourself. Do not be in a hurry. Even if you think you are alone, act as if someone is watching you.

"Herlwin, remember what I told you. Speak only if spoken

to. Keep your voice low. You are a monk, so you should be one of the quietest people on earth."

"Like Leof?"

"Aye."

"So we go to the manor house then?" Rhys asked. "And what do we do when we get there?"

Carlyle plucked a blade of grass and studied it. "What do you see?" he asked.

"A blade of grass."

Carlyle waved his arm in the air indicating the world around them.

Rhys stared at Carlyle before glancing about slowly. "Trees. Grass. Sky."

"When our Lord walked this earth, He taught his followers by speaking words they heard with their ears and doing miracles they saw with their eyes. But when He left the earth, He no longer spoke to their earthly senses. They had to learn to hear His voice with the ears of their hearts, to see Him with the eyes of their hearts."

Rhys cast a wary eye at Carlyle. "How do you see with your heart?"

"Can you see the wind? Nay, but you see the trees waving as the wind blows through them. Remember this; things that you see with your heart are more true than what you think you see with your eyes. And after that, know that the heaven-King will show you what your heart needs to see."

Rhys sat back and rubbed his chin.

"When we get to the manor," the monk continued patiently, "Herlwin and I will keep the attention on gathering alms for the poor, while you try to find and free Alayn. The rest is in the hands of God."

\* \* \*

From the road to Iconium, we could see a few angels moving about Edenton. There was nothing unusual about that. Zophar had been there for seventeen years watching over Rhys

136

while Dragon ruled the town through Acwellen. There was a sort of restless truce. We had not been ready for battle so we stayed away from Dragon. But Rhys had begun to draw Dragon's attention before he left, and we feared that his return would rouse the devils.

"I see no sign of Dragon," Haelstrum said.

"Perhaps the sight of us scared him away," Mycynn smiled fleetingly.

I observed, "It's unusually quiet."

Zophar unsheathed his sword. "Perhaps they have been warned that we are coming."

"Look!" Haelstrum pointed to the manor house. Running towards us was an angel-like spirit though it had the sallow skin and the sunken eyes of a devil. For a moment, I thought it was Bittenrood. I told the others to stay their swords, and I stepped forward to meet him. It was not Bittenrood, however, but a fallen angel much like him. Some paces behind the devil walked four heavily armed wraiths.

The devil waved his sword in the air as he reached us, yelling "Stop! Stop where you are!" He glanced back at the wraiths some distance behind him, before catching me by the shoulder. "Quick, tell me! Is it true that we may come back? Will the Creator forgive our rebellion if we swear allegiance?"

I looked into a face twisted with fear. "Do you wish to worship the Lord and obey Him fully?" I asked.

The devil let go of my shoulder as if it burned his hand. A change came over him. His eyes narrowed as fear turned to disdain. "Worship?" he said scornfully. "You want me to worship Him?"

"'There is no freedom apart from worship of the Creator," I said.

The wraiths came within twenty feet of us and stopped. The devil glanced back at the wraiths and glared at me as he took several steps back toward them.

"What do you want here?" demanded the devil.

I gestured to the three men in brown robes who had emerged from the forest and were walking toward the manor house. "We are guardians of these men."

"What do they want in Edenton?"

"They request food for the poor," said I.

"Poor?" he asked. "Poor? What do you know of the poor?" he cried. "These people you call poor live short little lives and then they die. Happy they be in death. But those of us who have nothing but living death, we be the poor!"

He panted like a dog for a few seconds; the panting stopped as quickly as it had begun. "Are you not a guardian of Edenton?" he asked Haelstrum.

"Nay."

The devil placed his sword back into his scabbard. "Beware! We do not care for monks. We do not care for the poor. And we do not care for your kind. So watch your step in Edenton and keep those you guard in line. When Dragon returns, and he could return any moment, he may well choose to devour all of you."

He turned away with the wraiths following. When they reached the manor house, I said hastily in a low voice, "I believe Dragon being absent is an opportunity given us by the Spirit. But the opportunity may pass quickly. Zophar, watch for Dragon, and warn us the moment you see him. I will watch over Rhys. Haelstrum and Mycynn guard your charges."

\* \* \*

It was late afternoon when the three men passed the first of Edenton's cottages. Rhys kept his head down and his eyes fixed on the stones in the street. He remembered a hundred times when he and Alayn had run past these same cottages. The men heard the shouts of children who pointed at the brown robes, but they did not look away from the road. The green lawn in front of the massive timber-frame manor house was empty. They knew, however, that much of the activity at the manor took place in the buildings and gardens behind the house, and those buildings and gardens were enclosed by a large hedge.

Rhys recognized the iron knocker on the massive oak door of the manor house. Ormod had forged it in his shop. Carlyle reached up and banged the knocker against the door three times. Rhys lowered his head and heard Herlwin draw in a deep breath. Carlyle took a half step back from the door and waited. The only sound they heard was the cry of a hawk overhead. Finally, Carlyle stepped forward and grasped the knocker again. But before he could bang it against the door, they heard the door bar being lifted from the inside. Carlyle lowered the knocker, and the door swung open.

In the doorway stood a tall, thin, gray-haired man in a brown linen tunic. The bottom of his wispy gray beard rested on his chest. Rhys recognized him as Lord Acwellen's house steward. He frowned at the three men and demanded impatiently, "What do you want?"

Carlyle made a half bow. "Kind sir, we are ministers to the poor and the hungry. We have come to the generous estate of Lord Acwellen to gather alms and food. Certainly, sir, Lord Acwellen would have some pity in his heart for those who have been left homeless and starving by the raiding parties from the sea."

The steward's frown was broken by an involuntary twitch of his left cheek, causing his left eye to blink. "Nay! We have no use for beggars. Now be gone with you!"

He moved back to close the door, but Carlyle stepped into the doorway so it could not be closed. "Certainly, sir, you have many concerns which leave you little time for the poor. But many have been left with nothing. We can take food to them, or they can come get it themselves. Which would you prefer? Which do you think Lord Acwellen would prefer?"

The steward's cheek twitched, and he scowled at Carlyle. "They would not dare come here for food," he snarled.

"Hunger makes men desperate, and who knows what desperate men will do?" Carlyle stepped back from the door and motioned for Herlwin and Rhys to follow him. "Deal with them yourself, if that is your choice. Surely Lord Acwellen will understand."

They turned away from the manor house. "Halt!" the steward called after them. The three stopped. "You will take what food the cook can spare. Nothing more. You'll tell any who takes food from you that they are not to come here begging food on threat of their life!"

Carlyle turned and bowed to the steward. "The lord's steward is most generous."

The steward led them into the great hall of the manor house. Rhys had heard about the inside of the building from Ormod. But it was larger than he had dreamed—big enough to hold a dozen cottages, he thought. Far above his head, great wooden beams stretched the width of the building. In the middle of the hall was a fire with a huge porridge kettle on it. The smoke from the fire floated up among the beams and disappeared through a hole in the roof. The floor was laid with smooth swept stones. Along one wall lay straw sleeping mats. Rhys assumed that they were for the servants. On the far end of the hall was a raised platform with tables and chairs. *Lord Acwellen and his family must eat there*, Rhys thought to himself.

The steward ordered them to wait at a bench next to the door. He crossed to the fireplace in the middle of the room. There a short, fat woman stirred porridge in the black kettle. When the steward spoke to her she looked up at him, then across the room at the three sitting on the bench. She scowled at them. Rhys wondered if all of Lord Acwellen's servants were required to make such faces. Herlwin looked at Rhys and raised his eyebrows.

The steward returned to them from the fire and said curtly, "Supper is being prepared. You may have what food is left over. You will wait here till everyone is finished." He turned to leave, then stopped and said, "Oh, the cook said there is a bag of leeks in the garden." He turned to two boys who were setting up tables and benches between the fire and the platform on the other end of the hall and said, "Ebert, come here." A boy about the age of ten walked quickly across the hall to the men. Rhys thought he recognized the boy from the village and quickly lowered his gaze hoping the boy would not recognize him.

"Take this man out to the garden to get the bag of rotting leeks," the steward said, pointing the boy toward Carlyle. Carlyle nodded at Rhys, then smiled at the boy, "Our young brother will go with you to get the leeks, Ebert."

Rhys stood, nodded to Carlyle, and looked at Ebert's feet, praying that the tonsure and the robe would be enough to keep the boy from recognizing him. Ebert bowed to Rhys, then turned and started across the hall with Rhys following.

Rhys tried to keep his head down as they crossed the stone floor, but he could not resist taking a few glances around the great hall. Along the walls near the platform, hung green and white woven banners with images of dragons and warriors. They passed several doors to private rooms on the edge of the hall. *Bed chambers for the lord and his family*, Rhys thought. They came to a door and stopped as two young ladies entered carrying bread. The first had long golden hair and green eyes. She caught her breath when she saw Rhys. The second girl, who had wavy red hair and freckles, squealed, "Oh!" Rhys realized he was staring and looked down. As they passed, he felt his face flush. "We've not seen brown-robed monks around here afore," Ebert whispered to him.

Behind the manor house were a number of small buildings, flower and vegetable gardens, and grape vines. They passed what Rhys guessed was the bake house, with the smell of freshly baked bread coming from it. Rhys tried to look into the next small stone building, but Ebert walked too quickly for him. Suddenly Ebert stopped. Rhys nearly ran into him. "There it be; that bag of rotting leeks. I don't know why you'd want it. The cook told us to pitch them to the pigs yesterday, but no one would."

Rhys reached down and started to lift the woven bag of leeks. But the rotted cloth they were wrapped in gave way, and leeks spilled out onto the ground. "I feared that," Ebert said. "I'll see if there be another cloth in the barn."

Rhys was grateful for the moment alone. He looked around

at the small buildings wondering which might hold the prisoners. He wandered over to a small wooden building. He glanced around, held his breath, then pushed the door open and peeked in. The building smelled of musty earth. When Rhys' eyes adjusted to the dark, he saw hand ploughs, shovels, and an axe. He stepped away from the building and looked back at the stable where Ebert had gone to look for a bag. There was no sign of Ebert.

Between the bake house and the small wooden building was the stone building they had passed too quickly for Rhys to look into. Rhys walked over to it and stood listening for voices. He heard none. He saw no sign of Ebert so he reached for the door and gave it a push. The door swung open with a creaking sound that Rhys despised. Rhys stepped inside the dark building and then gasped. From behind a large wooden barrel, Rhys saw a man's legs on the floor. *Is it Alayn?* Rhys' heart pounded as he stepped across the legs and looked down. It was not Alayn, but a much older man. He appeared to be asleep. Suddenly Rhys noticed the kegs of ale around him and realized he was in the brew house. The man was drunk.

Quickly Rhys left the brew house and walked back to the pile of leeks. Before looking around, he paused for a second over the leeks in case he was being watched. The only other building was a stone structure that stood beyond the garden. Seeing no sign of anyone, Rhys walked around the garden toward it. The building was the same length as the brew house but twice as wide. There were two doors in the front of the building spaced equally apart. On each door, near the top, was a small window.

Rhys had to stand on his tiptoes to see into the first window. The room had an earthy smell that reminded him of the stable at the abbey. All he could see was the room's dark ceiling, but he heard something stirring inside. He looked down and saw the door was barred and locked. Glancing about for something to stand on, Rhys found a stool nearby. The stool allowed him to see through the window, but he had to wait for his eyes to adjust to the darkness. After a moment he could see the outline of a wooden table and chair. There was a dark form in the corner of the room, but Rhys could not make out whether it was an animal or a man.

Rhys' heart began to race. He whispered, "Alayn?"

The black thing stirred then stopped. Rhys began to lose hope. "Alayn?" he whispered again.

The black thing stirred again. It stood up, and Rhys saw that it was a man. He took several slow, hesitant steps toward the window and the light.

"Rhys?" he asked.

# Chapter 17

## FLEEING THE DRAGON

"Alayn! Alayn, be it you?" Rhys asked. It was Alayn, Rhys realized. He knew the shape of Alayn's face under those thick, dark eyebrows. But Alayn had changed. There were dark lines around his eyes, and his once meaty face was much thinner. Alayn's clothes were dirty and hung loosely on him.

"Rhys, have they got you too?"

"We came to get you out, Alayn. Be you all right? What happened to you?"

Alayn started to speak, but lowered his head and coughed. He was silent for a moment, and Rhys saw tears on his cheeks. "A maiden servant be merciful to me, Rhys. She smuggles scraps of food from the kitchen. Her kindness has kept me." He looked up at Rhys with a dirty, streaked face. His hair was matted and tangled. The smell, like the smell of animal dung, made Rhys feel sick.

"Alayn, have no fear," Rhys told him. The words stuck in Rhys' throat, and a tear clung to his eye. He cleared his throat and whispered, "We'll get you out."

A movement caught Rhys' attention, and he turned to see Ebert coming out of the stable. "Someone's coming. I'll be back in a moment." Rhys stepped down from the stool, brushed off his robe, and strolled back to the leeks with his hands clasped in front of him. Ebert approached with his brow furrowed. He glanced at the keep and then at Rhys, trying to understand the connection.

Rhys tried to divert Ebert's attention. "I see you found a cloth for the leeks," he heard himself say in a Carlyle-like tone. "'Tis good."

Ebert, still looking from the keep to Rhys, replied, "Aye, sir. Please forgive the delay." An awkward moment of silence passed, then Ebert asked, "Be you talking to the prisoner?"

"We be brothers to those imprisoned as well as the free, Ebert." Rhys took the cloth from Ebert's hand, knelt down and began to pile the decomposing vegetables on it. Ebert stood watching. Rhys prayed for some way to make the boy leave him alone again. When he had finished putting the rotting stalks on the cloth, he asked, "Ebert, how much do you know about brown-robed monks?"

"You be the first I ever seen, sir."

"Did you know that we must pray very often?"

"Nay, sir."

"'Tis true, Ebert. And I've not prayed since early this morning. So I must pray now."

"Right now?" Ebert asked wide-eyed.

"Aye, Ebert."

Ebert stood staring at Rhys.

"Ebert."

"Aye, sir?"

"I need to pray for a while."

Ebert stood waiting as if to see some amazing sight.

"Alone, Ebert. I need to pray alone."

Ebert's face fell, but he turned and began to walk slowly back toward the stable. He had gone only a few steps when he looked back at Rhys, causing him to nearly miss the door and walk into the stable wall. Rhys bent over the sack of rotten leeks with his head bowed. He looked up just enough to see Ebert disappear into the stable. *Not very convincing*, Rhys thought to himself, *but it be the only thing that came to mind.*

Rhys got up and ran back to the keep.

"It only be a servant boy," he told Alayn.

"Rhys, what be your plan? Have you got the key?"

Rhys shook his head. "Do you know where it be?"

"The maiden told me the steward keeps it in a storage room, next to Lord Acwellen's bed chambers. I think Acwellen be gone. Can you get the key?"

Rhys thought about going into the manor house to look for the storage room. A few seconds passed; Alayn was watching him, but Rhys couldn't just wander about the manor house searching for a key. "I don't know if I can find it without getting caught," he told Alayn.

"The lock be too strong to break. You'll have to get the key to get me out. If you find the maiden with red hair, she may help you. But watch out for the steward!"

Rhys nodded.

* * *

I stood behind the manor house, watching Rhys. I glanced around; occasionally a devil passed, but they paid little attention to Rhys or me. Suddenly, Zophar appeared from around the corner of the manor house. He glanced about, then lowered his head and said with a quiet urgency, "Dragon is nearing Edenton with Acwellen's caravan!"

"How soon will he be here?"

"Half an hour, if he stays with Acwellen's caravan. Otherwise, he could be here any moment."

"Warn Haelstrum and Mycynn. Enter their world only if you must, but we have to get the men out of Edenton now. Once Dragon gets here, all could be lost!"

* * *

*Find the red-headed maiden*, Rhys told himself. He walked toward the door to the great hall where he had last seen the maiden. He stopped at the door, pondering what to do next. *Go on.* He reached over and pushed the door open and looked in. Just inside the door was the narrow hallway that led past the lord's private bed chambers. He stepped inside and moved quietly along the hallway. He stopped at the last bed chamber and peeked around the corner into the great hall.

The meal had ended. Servants were beginning to rise from the benches. Carlyle and Herlwin stood waiting to gather the leftover food. He did not see the maiden with the red hair. Rhys glanced back down the hallway. *One of these rooms may be the storage room with the key*, he thought. He noticed the door next to him was smaller than the other doors. Suddenly, Rhys heard someone approaching. He pushed on the door, and it opened; so he quickly slid inside and closed it quietly behind him.

Rhys held his breath until he heard the person pass. As his eyes adjusted to the darkness, he saw straw brooms, pots, and ladles and realized he was in the storage room. He looked around the walls to find a place where the key might be hung. He moved some brooms, but saw no key. In the corner were several wooden barrels. Rhys tried to move one, but it was too heavy. He knelt down and reached behind the barrel and felt for the key.

Suddenly, the door opened and the room's darkness fled. Rhys turned and saw the steward looking down at him.

"What are you doing, you thief?!"

Rhys started to get up, but the steward swung his foot at Rhys and it glanced off the side of his jaw. Pain shot through his face as he fell back against the wooden barrel.

"You come here talking of the poor and then try to rob us? Well, I'll teach you!"

*Get up!* the voice inside Rhys' mind screamed at him. He began to push himself up when the steward's foot caught him in the stomach. Rhys fell back against the wooden barrel. Out of the corner of his eye, Rhys saw the enraged steward grab an ax. Rhys raised his arm to shield himself from the blow. But before it came he heard a crack, and the steward crumpled to the floor next to Rhys. In the doorway, Herlwin lowered a broken chair.

"Come, Rhys! We must flee!" Herlwin said, pulling Rhys to his feet. "Acwellen is returning, and I fear this steward will waken in a foul mood!"

Rhys' legs were weak; he leaned against the wall and rubbed the blood from his face. "I cannot leave, Herlwin. Not till I find the key and release Alayn."

"Carlyle says we must leave at once."

"This be the room where they keep the key, Herlwin. But I can't find it. You and Carlyle go. I'll find the maiden with the red hair." Rhys stumbled from the room.

Herlwin followed him. "But Carlyle said…."

Rhys stepped out of the manor house and looked around. Ebert and another boy stared at him from the stable. A man coming out of the brew house stopped and stared at Rhys. Rhys no longer cared who saw him; there was no time for secrecy. He started toward the stable, then looked back to the garden where the leeks had been. There in the shadows stood the red haired maiden watching him. He ran to her. She started back from fear. He sank to his knees and held his hands out, imploring her. "Wait! Tell me where to find the key to the keep. Please. I beg you! I be Alayn's friend. I want to set him free. Please help us!"

She stared at the young man in the brown robe with blood running down his neck. Slowly, she shook her head. "I cannot help you."

"Please, please help me. I beg you!"

"I cannot."

"Why?"

There was sadness in the maiden's green eyes. "Because the key be not here. Crosnan has it, and he be with Lord Acwellen."

Rhys stared at her as he took in her words. Then he lowered his head to the ground, defeated.

A crowd began to gather in front of the stable as word spread of the strange young monk in the garden. Rhys felt hands under his arms pulling him up.

"Fair maiden, is there a way we can leave the manor

grounds from the garden?" Carlyle asked.

The young woman nodded and pointed to a white gate along the hedges behind the brew house. Carlyle and Herlwin started with Rhys toward the gate. But Rhys pulled free from their grasp and ran to the keep. Tears ran down his face as he looked in the prison window. "Alayn, I've failed! I've failed you. If you die here, it be all my fault."

"Nay, Rhys. I heard the maiden—the key be not here. Go, Rhys, less they get you too!"

Rhys sobbed so that he could not speak. But he reached through the small window and touched Alayn's stained cheek with his hand.

\* \* \*

I looked into the sky and saw what I had dreaded—a black-winged devil flying toward the manor house. Two more appeared, then a dozen flying demons came into sight.

"On guard!" I shouted. "Dragon comes!" I turned and backed toward the other angels with my sword raised. Zophar, Mycynn, Haelstrum and I formed a circle with our backs to each other.

Devils from the manor house quickly gathered around us as they heard of the disturbance among Lord Acwellen's servants. Winged devils dropped from the sky. A few angels from Edenton stood watching, wondering what was happening. Suddenly the devil that we first met when we entered Edenton pushed to the front of the crowd.

"What have you done?" he screamed. "I told you to keep your men in line! You broke the truce. Dragon will be angry, and we'll all be punished!"

Mycynn, who had little experience in battle, gripped his sword tightly and glanced to his side to see what Haelstrum was doing. Haelstrum held his sword with both hands over his chest. He gazed calmly at the panting devil in front of him and said, "You chose to not worship the Creator. You chose to be a slave to Dragon."

The devil screamed in rage and rushed at Haelstrum. Haelstrum swung his sword, severing the devil's head from its body. With a thousand screams the devils attacked us. We slashed and hacked. We cut, severed, ripped, and divided. Our blades were like fire. But the devils kept coming. We began to weaken from the weight of the devils' blows. A sword caught Mycynn in the chest and he fell.

We tightened the circle above him and continued to fight. A devil's blade glanced off Zophar's arm, and Haelstrum got a leg wound. We could not hold out much longer. I began to think the fight was lost when, without warning, the devils drew back. We lowered our swords.

"I had begun to think it was over," I said in a low voice.

Zophar looked into the sky above the manor house. "We have worse yet to face, Iothiel."

I turned and saw the huge beast, black as night, staring down at us from the top of the manor house. His eyes were like burning coals. His mouth, when opened, was like the door to hell itself. His feet were tipped with long, curved talons like those of a hawk.

"Why do you wield your swords in my domain?" he thundered at us.

Zophar and I stood side-by-side facing the dragon. Behind us, Haelstrum lifted the limp body of Mycynn. We knew that our only hope now was to flee if the opportunity arose.

I told Dragon, "We were set upon by your devils, and we defended ourselves. We did not strike first."

"Why have you come? What is your purpose here?" Dragon demanded, sending flames of fire to our feet.

My face burned from the heat, but I stood fast. "You will have to inquire of the Creator for our purpose. For it is from Him."

At this, rage filled Dragon. He breathed fire over us with a mighty roar. "You have come here to destroy me, but I will destroy you!" He raised his right front leg and opened the long talons to snatch us up.

We raised our swords to defend ourselves. As we did, a

brilliant light, like that of ten suns, lit the garden and nearly blinded Dragon and the devils. We turned and saw the mighty archangel, Gabriel, raising a sword of pure fire over his head. He was greater and more terrible than Dragon, and he shone like the sun, moon, and stars together.

"Stand fast, Dragon!" the angel commanded in a voice as big as the sea. "These are not yours. They belong to the Creator, and their service to Him is not finished."

Devils fled the angel's presence, running for shelter behind buildings and cottages throughout Edenton. The enraged Dragon thrashed the air with his tail. He growled and roared, but he did not approach us. We retreated under the sword of the great angel to the edge of Edenton, and there we found the men.

\* \* \*

The three men trudged through the gathering darkness of the forest north of Edenton. They pushed on in spite of their weariness because they knew it was best to get as far from Edenton as they could before darkness made traveling impossible. The men did not talk, but for the first mile an occasional sniffle came from Rhys. He wiped his face with his sleeve and stared at the ground in front of him. He could not remember leaving the garden through the white gate. Nor did he remember Carlyle leading them around Edenton to avoid being seen by the returning Acwellen and his thanes. He could only stare at the ground in front of him and walk.

Herlwin was relieved when Carlyle finally stopped their flight through the dark forest. They stretched out under a tree to rest though sleep did not come easily for Herlwin. He shifted about trying to find a place on the ground with no roots. He heard Carlyle rise and move away from them for midnight prayers. He heard the patter of raindrops in the tree top. He shifted again and said, "I've been lying here thinking about the meal at Acwellen's manor house. I was beginning to think that the meal would never end. You could certainly tell that the lord was not there the way those servants went on eating and eating. They had no intention of leaving much for the poor. Still, few things are more enjoyable than good food and fellowship."

Herlwin paused, but there was no response. "I'm sorry about your friend, Rhys," he added in a low voice.

What seemed a moment later, Herlwin opened his eyes and saw the leaves of the tree above him in the grey light. Herlwin sat up and looked around. "Carlyle not back from his morning prayers yet?"

There was no reply. He looked over to where Rhys had lain the night before and suddenly realized that Rhys was not there.

# Chapter 18

## THE TRYING OF THE HEART

When Rhys crept away from the sleeping monks, Gabriel and I followed. Haelstrum, the only other guardian to not have been sent to Orion, stayed behind to guard Carlyle and Herlwin.

As archangel, Gabriel has command over the guardians throughout the earth, and, thus, visits this sphere as he is needed. But he rarely stays long for he is frequently sought at his place in the heavens. When he is on earth, he often wraps himself in a robe to hide his shining countenance, allowing him to move about without drawing attention.

This night, Gabriel pointed to a dark form moving through the trees to our right and whispered, "The devils are drawn to the weak. Behold the despair in Rhys and how it has brought this devil to try him."

The devil, like those that had been at the burial of the monks, was unarmed. Gabriel stopped, letting Rhys and the devil move away from us. "The man is headed toward Iconium. Carlyle will not be there this time to turn him from the devil's lies. Rhys alone must take the test. Allow no harm to his body—but remember that he must win the fight on his own."

"Guard him well," he told me. "He will be weakened by

hunger a few more days."

The next moment, I was alone in the dark woods.

\* \* \*

Leof put the last of the radishes in a small pot of porridge hanging over the fire. Hermes hopped about the shadows in the courtyard, before taking flight. Leof straightened up and turned around. Coming through the abbey gate he saw Carlyle and Herlwin. Carlyle was limping, and Herlwin followed, slump-shouldered like an old bear.

Herlwin gave Leof a weary smile. "We feared for you. We saw the reeve riding this way."

Leof nodded to them. "Rest you by the fire. I'll get the bowls for porridge and call the brothers."

The travelers settled by the fire. In a moment, Leof reappeared with two monks. "Dunstan and Guthram returned to help with the wheat harvest and the restoration of the abbey."

The brothers nodded to one another. Carlyle said quietly, "We are returning from Edenton. Rhys left us without notice the night before last."

"I know," Leof replied.

Carlyle raised an eyebrow.

"He was here yesterday," Leof continued. "He told me about Alayn before taking his bow into the woods."

"Will he be coming back?" asked Carlyle.

"He would not say. I tried to give him some of this porridge. 'Tis the last of it. He would only take a few bites. He knows there is no more till the wheat harvest next week. He took his bow and went out the back gate."

Herlwin frowned and looked at Carlyle.

\* \* \*

Lying devils, like the one now following Rhys, are the most dangerous devils of all. Lucifer was the first lying devil. He lied to Adam and Eve in the Garden of Eden. The devils' lies are intended to break the heart with anger, suspicion, and fear. They seek to separate friends and kinsmen. Their lies are more destructive than the sword.

I guessed that the lying devil that came to Rhys intended to poison the bond between he and Carlyle. Rhys' youth required Carlyle's wisdom. Beyond that, devils always question the goodness of God. From the moment they fell from heaven, they have questioned the Almighty's kind intent toward His creatures. For them, the question is a mystery so why not force it on the minds of weak men? They knew as well as I that Rhys would need faithful dependence on God to defeat Dragon.

This devil and I followed Rhys to the abbey and, eventually, into the forest beyond the abbey. I could not read Rhys' thoughts. At the abbey, he spoke little to Leof, and what he did say did not reveal his intentions. Since he took the bow and quiver of arrows, I assumed he was going to hunt. But whether he intended to return to the abbey, I could not tell.

The devil, a shadowy form with a pale, watery face, stared unblinkingly at Rhys. When the devil spoke, I heard his voice in my head as if it were one of my own thoughts though his mouth did not move. "I have permission," the husky voice said as we followed Rhys through the back gate of the abbey.

"Speak your lies," I said aloud. "But make one move to harm his body, and I will send you to the abyss."

The devil swayed slightly as if a breeze had passed. "Words are all I need to do my work. One partly innocent question is all it takes to sow doubt, wound the heart, or set one against another."

I made no reply. The devil shifted its gaze to Rhys as he crossed the meadow and entered the forest.

\* \* \*

Leof, Dunstan, and Guthram had begun cutting small trees for rebuilding the roofs of the buildings, beginning with the chapel and scriptorium. Now Carlyle and Herlwin joined them in the work. But since they had little food, their strength was limited. They would work for a bit, rest, and work some more. Every day Leof went to the wheat field to see if the wheat was ripe and ready to harvest. Each day he would return with Hermes on his shoulder and shake his head.

In the meantime Rhys wandered beside the stream that ran along the route to Carlyle's cottage. He was able to find deer tracks in the soft stream bank. But when the tracks disappeared on the harder ground away from the stream, he became discouraged and wandered aimlessly for several hours.

The devil spoke its lies patiently, a little at a time. It began with hunger—if God cared for Rhys, why would He let Rhys go hungry? Why would He let the monks go hungry? And with each pang of hunger, Rhys would be reminded of the question. Couldn't God provide food like He did with the loaves and fishes? Why is it those who follow Him, like the monks, go hungry, while those like Acwellen have all the food they want?

Rhys found himself back at the stream. This time, he didn't see any tracks so he took a drink and sat down, staring across the stream into the forest while the questions continued to haunt him. If Carlyle was a wise man, why did he take them on such a wild, dangerous mission? If Carlyle heard God's voice, why did their attempt to save Alayn fail? Why would God send them on such a task, knowing that the key was not there? Finally, the forest faded along with the evening sun. Rhys curled up under the boughs of an evergreen and fell asleep. When he awoke in the morning, he was damp, cold, and still hungry.

The second day in the forest was much the same. A few tracks by the stream were the only sign of deer he could find. He couldn't remember how many days he had been hunting, but he thought it had been two, maybe three. He had only eaten the few berries he could find. He was weak. His belt was too loose even though he had tightened it to the last notch. His eyes felt like they were starting out of his head like a toad's.

Late in the afternoon, Rhys stopped where a bit of sunlight

shone through the trees. He could go no further. He lay in the grass and wondered if someone would come his way years later and find his bones. The voice in his mind stopped for a moment, and he fell asleep.

\* \* \*

"Trying to kill him, are you?" I said to the devil.

The devil seemed pleased with my statement, as if it were a complement. He almost seemed to smile. I heard his words in my mind, "Death works best from the inside out." The devil turned its gaze back to Rhys, "He is beginning to respond to my efforts."

As the devil concentrated on Rhys, I moved slowly back into the woods. I needed to walk and think, to find some way to break the devil's power over Rhys. Keeping my eyes on the devil, I moved slowly around the trees where Rhys slept. When I had come all the way around and stood behind the devil again, something to my right caught my attention. I swung my head around as Zophar placed his hand on my arm and put a finger to his lips. He motioned for us to move away from the devil.

Zophar whispered, "How long will this go on?"

"Until Rhys refuses to believe the lies."

"We can't intervene?"

"Gabriel warned me against intervening unless he is threatened physically."

"If the devil can lie to him," Zophar said, "can't we tell him the truth?"

"We do poorly what only the Whispering Voice does well."

"A distraction then—certainly we can do that?"

When I returned to Rhys, the devil had begun to weave a dark dream and whisper it into Rhys' soul. Rhys dreamed of walking through a gloomy forest. Faces came to him; first the face of Abbot Wilfrid as he lie on the ground in the stable; then Petrus and Gildon, silent in death; and Alayn, pale and thin peering from the bars in Acwellen's keep. The murky faces peered at Rhys from the forest shadows. His heart pounded as he began to run, fleeing the faces.

As the darkness closed in about him, he saw the light of a cottage ahead. He hurried to the door and opened it. It was the cottage that Rhys had been raised in. He saw Alayn standing by the fire. Alayn smiled at Rhys and then turned away. As Rhys looked at him, it became apparent that it was not Alayn after all. The man was older and heavier than Alayn. *It must be Ormod*, Rhys thought. *I'll go to him and ask him where Alayn went.* But when Rhys went to the man, to his horror, it was not Ormod but Baldric.

In Baldric's right hand was a large bloody knife. Rhys looked down. At Baldric's feet lay a dead goat. The sight made him feel sick. "Why did you kill it?" Rhys asked.

"Grim requires it."

"Why? Is he hungry?"

"Every god requires a sacrifice—even Carlyle's. Why do you think Carlyle took you to Edenton? You were to be his sacrifice." Rhys stared at the animal on the ground and felt fear inside him growing. Baldric grinned wickedly at him and raised the bloody knife. Rhys wanted to scream "No!" but the word would not come out.

Rhys opened his eyes and saw the dim gray of twilight in the branches above him. He blinked and sat up. The dim light made him feel all the more alone. He remembered the dream and wondered if it was the reason his heart pounded so hard. *I must have slept for an hour or more.*

He heard the rustling of a tree branch. The sound came from the trees in front of him. Rhys' heart began beating wildly again. He pushed himself to his feet with his hands and, crouching near the ground, picked up his bow and quiver. The sound stopped. Rhys prayed that he could see it, whatever it was. He slid the quiver over his shoulder and placed an arrow on the string. It took another step, and he saw it. The head and shoulders of a large deer were barely visible between two trees thirty feet away. Rhys' muscles relaxed only slightly. He was relieved to be the hunter rather than the hunted. He judged the distance to the deer and slowly raised the bow. The deer took another step forward. Rhys focused on the spot, just behind the shoulder, where he wanted the arrow to go. He pulled back the string, took a breath and held the string for a second—then released it. The deer leaped a half second after the arrow hit. It crashed into the darkness and disappeared.

Rhys ran as fast as he could toward the sounds of the fleeing deer. He tripped over a rock. But he got up and ran again hoping the deer would fall, and he could find it. He veered to his left to avoid briers, but not before they scraped his face. Rhys stopped and listened. There was a crash just ahead of him. He ran past thinning trees straight into a clearing and stopped.

\* \* \*

Zophar and I, followed by the lying devil, ran after Rhys. The voice of the devil came to me, "You intervened. You woke my subject just as the deer happened by."

"We did not intrude into your lying," I replied aloud while thinking, *Nor did we anticipate this dash through the forest.*

We came suddenly upon a clearing and gazed at the scene in front of us.

\* \* \*

Though it was nearly dark, Rhys saw the deer lying in the clearing with the broken arrow shaft sticking out of its side. Two men walked toward the deer, before stopping and staring at Rhys. The skinny one Rhys recognized immediately. He was the Grim worshipper who had threatened Rhys and Elene on the Grim hill.

At the same moment, Rhys heard someone cry out from the edge of the clearing. He glanced to his left and saw a boy tied by his wrists to a tree.

* * *

Three armed devils and a wraith stood behind the men in the clearing. An angel guardian stood next to the boy. Though there were five evil spirits and only three angels, the lying devil was unarmed and would not fight. So the odds were close enough to give me confidence. There was a moment in which neither man nor spirit moved. Then Zophar and I drew our swords.

* * *

"Help me!" the boy cried. It was Ebert, the boy who had helped Rhys at Acwellen's manor house. Rhys had only a moment to decide what to do. He didn't think the Grim worshippers would let him have the deer. And Ebert, who was apparently their prisoner, had been kind to him at the manor house. Rhys ran to him and using his hunting knife, cut the cord that bound his hands to the tree. The two men yelled and began running toward them. Rhys glanced back at the deer for a second, then turned and ran into the forest with Ebert behind him.

Rhys ran back the way he had come, toward the stream that led back to the abbey.

"Uhff!" Ebert tripped and went down hard.

Rhys stopped and ran back. "Come on! They'll catch us!"

"I can't run with me hands tied together!"

Rhys pulled out his knife and sawed through the cord that held Ebert's hands. He could hear someone making their way through the forest, but they sounded a ways off.

"They'll not be coming," Ebert whispered. "Least not the fat one. He couldn't keep up. And the other be none too eager—he seen what you done to that deer."

* * *

Zophar and I and Ebert's angel guardian covered the two

as they fled into the forest. However, the lying spirit followed; his power wasn't broken. He came slipping through the trees, the unblinking eyes staring at us and then at Rhys. The sight of the devil sickened me. I had hoped to be through with him.

* * *

"I've seen this skinny one afore," Rhys whispered. "We'll go on quietly till we be sure he'll not find us."

They went on more slowly, Rhys picking his way as well as he could and listening for footsteps. When they came to the stream, he stopped, and they both had a drink. Rhys sat back and looked at Ebert in the dark. The boy's tunic was soiled, his eyes appeared to be swollen from crying, and his face was smeared with dirt-streaked tears. "How'd you get caught by them?" Rhys asked.

"I run away from the manor house because of the prisoner; the steward caught me smuggling food to him. So he beat me. It be not the first time, see?" Ebert turned his back to Rhys and pulled down the tunic. His shoulders showed welts from the whippings he had suffered.

"But I don't want to fear the steward. All the servants be afraid of him. I want to be a thane when I grow up. Like Acwellen's thanes, only I want to fight for a good lord. And I can't become a thane if I be afraid of a steward. Can I?"

"I guess not," Rhys said.

"So then I come looking for you, when Bony and Fatty found me instead. And when you came chasing that deer, I didn't recognize you at first. Where be your robe?"

"I wore the robe only as a disguise to get into the manor house. I be no monk."

"A thane then?"

"Nay."

Ebert was clearly disappointed. "Aethelwynn thought you be someone important," he said to console himself.

"Aethelwynn?"

"The red-haired maiden," Ebert said. "You asked her to

161

help you get the prison key when you were there in the brown robe."

"Aye. Well, the maiden dreams. I be nothing more than what you see."

"But you use a bow. Commoners don't use bows."

"A lord showed me how to use the bow at my father's smith shop," Rhys said bitterly. "It has brought me little— more grief than good."

Ebert was silenced by Rhys' sharp reply. The two sat for a minute, staring at the ground and listening to frogs croaking along the stream. Rhys finally said, "Go to sleep. At first light I'll send you to the abbey."

"I be too hungry to sleep," Ebert complained.

"You'll get used to it."

"You'll not be going to the abbey?"

"They've not enough food for everyone."

"Where will you go?"

Rhys made a nod toward the east. "Maybe I'll go to the sea and become a fisherman."

\* \* \*

"So what do we do now?" asked Zophar.

I ignored Zophar's question. I had no idea what to do, but I would not show discouragement, for it only inspired the devil. *Steady*, I told myself, for all I wanted to do at that moment was to end this trial by putting my sword through that lying spirit. Zophar sighed and folded his arms across his chest.

Afriel, Ebert's guardian, said in a low voice, "Whatever happens, I thank you that your charge intervened in the circumstances of this boy. He may well have been hung as an example to those who run away."

I nodded. "In Ebert's freedom we can rejoice."

# Chapter 19

## THE MESSAGE

When Ebert woke the next morning, he found Rhys sitting nearby with his back to a tree. "'Tis light enough to travel," Rhys told Ebert. "Better start for the abbey."

Ebert wished for some warm porridge, but he knew better than to complain.

"You helped me at Acwellen's manor house," Rhys continued, "and I've helped you here. We've no debt to the other. Shall we part friends?"

Ebert nodded and swallowed before saying, "I didn't mean to repeat what Aethelwynn said about who you be. I didn't know it would upset you."

"Never mind. Go. There may be something to eat at the abbey."

Ebert stood and felt a pouch hanging around his neck. "Oh, I forgot." He removed the leather pouch and handed it to Rhys. "I started to tell you last night, but, um...I mean, when the maiden, Aethelwynn, heard that I planned to run away, she asked me to find you and give you this."

Rhys got to his feet and took the pouch. Inside, he found a rolled piece of parchment paper.

"Can you read?" asked Ebert.

"A little, but I'll need some help with this. I see the words *Loafmas* and *Alayn*."

"They say at the manor house '*the only secrets here be the ones we don't yet know.*'" Ebert flashed a quick grin, before turning serious. "At Loafmas, Acwellen intends to have another contest. He intends to have Alayn fight, only it won't be a fair match. He'll fight one of the lord's thanes."

Rhys stood as still as if his breath had left his body.

"The only other prisoner be a man that fought and killed two of Acwellen's thanes. But he refuses to fight Alayn. So Alayn will fight one of the lord's thanes. And the prisoner will be hung after Loafmass."

Ebert continued, "The maiden Aethelwynn wants you to save Alayn. You're the only one who has tried."

Rhys stared at Ebert. "But there only be a few days...."

Ebert waited, wondering if he should start for the abbey in case they had food. But it didn't seem right to leave Rhys in such low spirits.

"Perhaps, if we could we find Bors...." Rhys wondered aloud.

"Did you say Bors? That be the name of the prisoner they be going to hang. He killed some of Acwellen's men when they were returning from their hunting trip and you were leaving the manor house."

"What?"

"A man killed two of Acwellen's thanes before they stopped him. His name, they said, was Bors."

"Did you see him?" Rhys cried.

Ebert nodded.

"Did he have a scar where the eyebrow should be?"

Ebert nodded again. "The rumor be that he heard about the burning of the abbey. And out of rage, he attacked the reeve and his thanes. Killed two of them before they stopped him. He'll be hung after Loafmas, they say."

\* \* \*

I groaned when I heard Bors' name. Zophar looked at me. I could hear the devil's voice in my head telling Rhys that there was nothing he could do. Maybe Bors was getting what he deserved, the devil told him; after all, his hatred of Acwellen had caused him to kill two men. And Alayn—had he not teased Rhys for all their years? Perhaps this was God's judgment on them both. Maybe Acwellen was more like God than Rhys' had realized. The only thing Rhys could do was go as far away from Edenton as he could.

"Pray the Spirit is speaking to Rhys," I told the angels. "And Rhys can hear Him over that devil's lies."

\* \* \*

"Mother Mary!" Rhys swore with such anger that Ebert began to cry. Rhys turned away, his own eyes clouded. He cursed, picked up a limb, and struck it so hard against a tree that it broke into pieces. Rhys swore bitterly. The cursing and the anger sounded to Ebert like blasphemy and scared the boy such that he feared they would both be struck by God in His anger. The boy ran sobbing into the forest.

Rhys glared after him and cursed some more. He cursed the day he was born, he cursed his luck, he cursed the smith shop, he cursed the ill-fated trip to help Alayn. He thought about cursing more; he thought of cursing God—He was in charge of it all, wasn't He?—but Rhys thought of the woman who had mothered him, and he stopped. He did not want to dishonor her memory by doing something that would have horrified her. Rhys knees buckled. *Tis too much bad luck*, he said, addressing God in his thoughts from his hands and knees. He assumed the cursing had gotten him the attention of the Almighty. *Bors was our last hope and now You've taken him.*

But then the fog of anger and frustration in Rhys' head lifted and there came into his mind a voice as clear and sure as if Ebert had spoken. *Bors was trying to do what I called you to do. I let him fail, because I made you the Lord Protector of Edenton.*

Rhys stopped. He looked around to see who had spoken, but there was no one there. He knew that this voice came from someplace or someone different than all his confusing thoughts. Was this the Voice? Was this what Carlyle called listening with the ears of your heart? Rhys couldn't say whether the voice was deep like Ormod's or childlike. He couldn't describe the sound of the voice, only that he was sure what had been said. And he could not explain why, but he believed this to be the voice of his true Father who made and loved him without rebuke.

A wall inside Rhys broke and some kind of light came flooding in. For the first time in his life, he sensed the strength of the Creator's design within him. His complaints and anger disappeared like a leaf caught in a stream. All of his failures as a smith didn't matter anymore; they simply didn't matter. He knew now what he was made for, and there was nothing else to do, nothing else made sense. These words, like Carlyle's words, while hard, were true, and Rhys must no longer believe otherwise. He felt a sense of relief and joy, though it seemed an odd moment for joy.

Carefully positioned behind a tree, Ebert eyed Rhys, expecting at any moment for the young man to disappear in a blaze of fire and smoke. Instead, Rhys appeared to have gone mad, wiping tears from his eyes and smiling. Ebert stepped out from behind the tree and gazed warily at Rhys.

"Shall I go to the abbey?" He waited a moment. Rhys did not respond, so Ebert said, "I'll go to the abbey and see if they have food, if that be acceptable."

Rhys glanced in Ebert's direction but did not appear to see him. Rhys took a deep breath, stiffened his back and turned in the direction of the camp they had escaped the night before.

"Where you headed?"

"I know where there be enough meat to feed the brothers and us."

Rhys picked up his bow and quiver and began to run. Ebert ran after him. They quickly covered the ground they had walked the night before. Ebert was so worried that he forgot his hunger. Rhys stopped and stood staring into the clearing, his breath coming in gasps. Ebert caught up with him and saw the gutted and skinned deer hanging from a tree branch. The two men were sitting around a small fire eating strips of the cooked meat.

"What are you going to do?" Ebert asked.

"Stay behind me."

\* \* \*

I drew my sword as we approached the clearing—I knew there would be at least three devils and a wraith ahead. But there was a commotion behind me, and I turned to see the lying devil point to Rhys.

"I had him," the devil screamed. "He was mine! You interfered!"

Zophar poked his sword in the devil's chest. "Speak no more. We've had enough of your mutterings."

\* \* \*

Rhys took a deep breath and walked out into the clearing toward the two men. The skinny one saw Rhys first and stood up. The fat one turned around and, upon seeing Rhys, stood up as well and asked, "What do you want?"

"That be my deer," Rhys said, stopping within twenty feet of the men. "I shot it, and I come to claim it."

"That be our boy," the fat one said, pointing to Ebert, "afore you stole him."

"You have no claim over him," Rhys replied.

"He belongs to Lord Acwellen, and he run away. Give us the boy, and we'll give you some of the meat."

"I am the son of Lord Erlan, the one Acwellen murdered. I am lord of Edenton and all that is in the manor house, and of Acwellen himself. Ebert be my subject, and that be my deer."

The fat man's belly shook with a burst of laughter. He grinned and looked around at the skinny man, but the skinny one didn't smile. Staring at Rhys, the skinny one said, "I fear 'tis true, and his god be strong. We'll not want to anger his god again. Remember what happened last time."

The fat man frowned and swore as he looked back at Rhys. "You want this deer, boy? You come over here and take it. I'll not be coward to the likes of you."

There is some question as to what happened next. The devils claim that we angels allowed ourselves to be seen by the men. It is not my place to say what the heathen men saw. What I know is that Zophar, Afriel, and I stood in the clearing guarding Rhys and Ebert. Suddenly, the fat man's eyes went wide and his knees went wobbly. He turned to the skinny man and tried to speak, but nothing came out; all he could do was point to the deer.

Rhys had no idea what caused the odd behavior in the fat man, but he was quick enough to seize the opportunity. "For goodwill," he said. "I'll give you the flank of the deer. The rest goes to the brothers."

The skinny man took a knife from his belt and cut the deer down. He cut off a flank before lifting the remaining deer and carrying it to a grassy place in front of Rhys. Rhys waited till the skinny man moved away from the deer and then put his bow over his head and shoulder. He motioned for Ebert, and the two of them lifted the deer.

"You there!" the skinny man called. "Let this pact be kept between us and no others."

Rhys nodded as he and Ebert lifted the deer and carried it from the clearing.

Ebert grinned. "I've not had meat since they killed the old boar a month ago! Bread be all I had, and I finished that yesterday. It doesn't stay in your belly like meat."

The brothers spent two days repairing the roofs on the abbey buildings. On the second day, however, Dunstan nearly fainted while climbing on the frame for the new roof of the scriptorium. So they decided to stay on the ground, where fainting was not as dangerous, until after the wheat harvest when they could have regular meals again. In the meantime,

Leof found a few berry bushes and gathered enough so that each brother could eat a handful. The rest he took to the village to give to the small children playing near the road.

On his way back to the abbey, Leof stopped to rest and pray under the shade of a tree. He sat gazing at the grass, the wheat field, and the patches of white clouds above. Hermes hopped about pecking at the grass and scratching the earth for worms. Leof watched the bird and wondered at the freedom of such a simple creature—freedom from worries and cares of this earth. *Neither do they toil nor spin*, Leof thought, *and yet look how God cares for them*. He looked across the wheat field imagining the lilies that the Lord had mentioned in His sermon on the mountain. But what caught his eye were two figures walking toward the back of the abbey carrying something between them. *Could it be the Lord?* Leof wondered. He stood and stared. One looked like Rhys, but the other was just a boy. *Could Rhys have gotten a deer?* Leof called to Hermes and headed back to the abbey at a lively pace.

Rhys and Ebert lay the deer on the large stones near the cooking fire in the abbey courtyard. Within minutes the five brothers had gathered around them. Herlwin swept Rhys off his feet in a bear-like hug. "Why did you leave your good friends to wander in the forest?" he said with the air of one offended. "Me thinks I would never see you again!"

"Quite a hunt," Carlyle said. "You got a deer and a boy."

Herlwin looked at Ebert. "What be this? Our little friend from the manor house in Edenton come to visit us?"

Guthram was busy adding wood to the fire so they could cook the venison. Ebert smiled and bowed to the brothers, but his thoughts were on how quickly the venison would be ready to eat.

"The deer ran into the camp of the Grim worshippers. I found Ebert from the manor house there."

Hoping to keep the conversation moving, Ebert added, "I ran away from the manor house, sir. The maiden Aethelwynn sent a message for Rhys." Ebert forgot the conversation, and he glanced at the deer. He knew it impolite to ask, but he was too hungry to care, "Be it cooked soon?"

Leof and Dunstan took a couple of iron bars that had been pulled from the rubble and propped the ends on stones, so the bars lay across the fire. They placed the deer on the bars.

Rhys continued, "When I saw Ebert last night, I cut him loose, and we ran. I went back for the deer this morning."

"And the Grim worshippers just gave you the deer?" asked Carlyle.

"Nay," Rhys looked at Carlyle for a moment, wondering how to explain what happened. "I told them the truth—that Acwellen murdered my father, and I be the true lord of Edenton."

Ebert added, "Bony got scared right off. Fatty was ready to fight, but something scared the devil out of him so he couldn't even speak."

Carlyle arched an eyebrow and stared, but Herlwin raised a cup of water, "To the Lord Protector's hunting skills—we have mead if you don't miss the honey or ale without the barley and hops."

"What is this message from the maiden?" Carlyle asked.

Rhys took the parchment from the leather bag and handed it to Carlyle. "Alayn'll be forced to fight in a contest to the death at Loafmas."

All movement stopped, and every eye turned to Rhys. "There be something else. Ebert says that Bors be Acwellen's prisoner. He attacked the reeve's thanes and killed two before being caught. They say he'll be hung after Loafmas."

There was a long silence broken only by the chirping of birds in the courtyard. "You saw Bors?" Carlyle asked Ebert.

"Aye, sir. He be the one missing an eyebrow?"

Carlyle nodded.

"Mother Mary!" Herlwin gasped.

Carlyle slowly raised the parchment and read aloud the words from it.

*"I write to the monk who requested my help in finding the key to Alayn's prison. Since I had not the key, I was unable to help you then. Now I write to ask you for help on Alayn's behalf.*

*At the festival of Loafmas, Lord Acwellen will again have a contest of prisoners. It is said that Alayn, the lord's most long standing prisoner, will fight the captain of the thanes.*

*I write to you on the fourth day of August. Only one week remains till the contest that ends Loafmas. If you have any means of coming to Alayn's aid, I beg you to do it now."*

*Aethaelwynn*

"Loafmas be in two days," Rhys said.

Carlyle looked up from the parchment. "'Tis time enough to get to Edenton."

"And what'll we do when we get there?" Rhys asked.

"I have Petrus' sword!" Herlwin cried. "We'll get quarterstaffs for the brothers!" His suggestion was met with a thoughtful silence.

Dunstan said, "The least we should do is go and pray for his soul."

"We can't let them hang Bors without an appeal for mercy. Would not Acwellen hear us out if we went to him?" Leof asked.

"What do you think?" Carlyle replied. "Did his men give Father Wilfrid the chance to appeal?"

* * *

"Do you think Rhys is ready?" Mycynn asked. We stood in the abbey courtyard with six other angels, including Zophar, Haelstrum, and Afriel.

"It depends on what is in the heart," I said. "And only God knows that for sure."

Zophar said, "We can't go back to Edenton without a fight. Had it not been for Gabriel, we would have been destroyed the last time we were there."

"All the devils in Wessex cannot thwart the Creator's plan," I said. "For the last seventeen years we have longed for the moment when Edenton would be set right. Perhaps the time has come."

* * *

After giving thanks for the food, the brothers cut off strips of the venison and ate in silence. Then they sat around the fire letting the food settle in their shrunken bellies as the shadows crept across the courtyard.

Carlyle finally broke the silence, "Whatever happens in Edenton, I do not think we shall prevail fighting Acwellen's thanes with quarterstaffs. Just as Rhys went into the camp of the Grim worshipers with truth, so we must go to Edenton."

"All the same," Herlwin said, "last time I found a chair. This time I'd rather have a quarterstaff with me."

Carlyle said to Rhys, "Have you heard of John the Baptizer, the Christ's cousin?"

Rhys nodded.

"A brother in Exeter wrote a story; I copied the manuscript, about how John in the afterlife is imprisoned in hell, and he sees our crucified Lord coming to set the captives free—just as you go to Edenton to set the captives free."

Herlwin cried, "O that we had this manuscript and could read John's story. Methinks it would give us hope for this adventure."

Carlyle eyes narrowed as if he gazed upon some distant land, and he began,

> *"Then the Lord of mankind hastened to his*
> *journey; the heavens' protector would demolish and lay*

*low the walls of hell and, most righteous of all kings,
carry off the stronghold's populace. For that battle he
gave no thought to helmet-wearing warriors, nor was
his will to lead armoured fighting men to the
stronghold gates. But the locks and the bars fell from
those fortifications and the king entered in; onward he
advanced, Lord of all the people, the multitudes'
Bestower of glory.*

*The exiles came crowding, trying which of them
might see the victorious Son—Adam and Abraham,
Isaac and Jacob, many a dauntless man, Moses and
David, Isaiah and Zacharias, many patriarchs,
likewise too a concourse of men, a host of prophets, a
throng of women and many virgins, a numberless tally
of people."*

*John then saw the victorious Son of God come with
kingly majesty to hell; the man of sorrowing heart then
recognized the coming of God's self. He saw the doors
of hell brilliantly gleaming which long since had been
locked and shrouded in darkness; that servant was in
ecstasy.*

*Boldly then, and undaunted before the multitude,
the leader of the stronghold's inhabitants called out
and spoke to his kinsman and with these words
greeted the longed for visitor:*

*'Thanks be to you, our Prince, because you were
willing to seek out us sinful men since we have had to
languish in these bonds.'*[1]

At that moment, Rhys knew that the Lord of all lords had
entered his heart just as He had entered hell's gates. *So that's
it...that's what a real lord does*, Rhys thought. *He sets captives free.*

"You despaired after our first attempt to help Alayn,"
Carlyle told Rhys. "From all appearances, it seemed that we

had failed. But if we had not gone the first time, we would not have met Ebert or Aethaelwynn. And we would not be going back to Edenton to rescue Alayn now."

"You see, 'tis in God's hand."

# Chapter 20

## THE GATE

The next morning we set our faces toward Edenton. The men split into three groups to make it easier to move through the forest unnoticed. Herlwin and Guthram went first, accompanied, of course, by their guardians. About a half hour later, Carlyle left with Dunstan and Leof. Haelstrum and the other two guardians went with them. Since Rhys knew the way to the hiding place outside of Edenton better than the others, he went last with Ebert. Therefore, if Herlwin or Carlyle weren't sure of the way, they could stop and wait for Rhys to catch up with them.

Before we left, I sent Zophar to Sargon in Iconium with a message for Gabriel. Zophar caught up with Afriel, Ebert's guardian, and me before we had been in the forest an hour.

"You have delivered the message to Sargon?" I asked.

"He wings his way toward heaven."

"To Edenton then and to Dragon."

* * *

The men spent the night at the cave. They ate cold meat and bread for they did not want to risk starting a fire. They left the next morning after prayers and by late afternoon they reached the hiding place on the edge of Edenton. As they rested under the tree, they could smell the Loafmas bread baking and hear people talking on the market road. Rhys looked at Carlyle who lay with his eyes closed and chest rising and falling slowly. Rhys wanted to ask what he thought they should do, but decided it was best to let him rest. Herlwin sat down beside Rhys and began asking him which merchants he thought might be displaying their wares.

"Be there more than one ale brewed in Edenton?" he asked.

"The only brew house is behind the manor, near the back gate," Rhys said in a hushed tone before pausing. "I've been thinking about that back gate you and Carlyle brought us out of last time. I'm going to go around back of it to see if it be open there. Would you tell Carlyle when he wakes?"

Herlwin raised an eyebrow. "You'll not get into danger, will you?"

"Seems there would be less danger going in the back than the front," Rhys replied.

Herlwin nodded. "I'll tell him. Quiet like a mouse now."

\* \* \*

The heavens over Edenton had changed since our last visit. Because of Loafmas, the town was overflowing with angels and devils moving about one another in an uneasy truce. *A good sign*, I thought, *the more spirits, the less likely we are to be seen by Dragon.* At that moment, Dragon climbed to the top of the manor house and thrashed his tail about nervously. I wondered if he was haunted by the memory of Gabriel appearing in Edenton.

"I've never faced a dragon before," Afriel whispered.

"They live on the evil in a man's heart and rule by overpowering strength," I told him, "That is why Rhys cannot win this battle simply by the sword."

"And what if he does not win?"

I turned and looked at Afriel to see if he were serious in this question. There was nothing in his face that suggested otherwise, so I replied, "Our purpose is to obey in times both evil and good. The rest is up to the Creator. We do not consider, *what if?*"

Afriel nodded and gazed at Dragon on the manor roof.

\* \* \*

Rhys slipped across the road and made his way quietly through the trees toward the back of the manor house. When he came to the edge of the trees he stopped. There were thirty feet of open ground between the trees and the hedges by the white gate. He watched for movement at the gate, but saw no one. He held his breath, wondering how long to wait before making a dash for the gate to see if it was locked.

\* \* \*

Zophar and I stood behind Rhys, facing the back of the manor house. We could see a guard near the gate on the other side of the hedge. But Rhys couldn't see the guard, I guessed, for he appeared to be getting ready to run across the open ground between the trees and the gate. I glanced around, looking for some way to stop him. To my right, I recognized an angel named Solon. But to my left, coming directly toward us were three devils, two armed with swords; the other held a scythe often used by devils when an innocent man is about to be murdered. Zophar drew his sword.

"Hold steady, Zophar," I whispered. He looked at me with doubt in his eyes, but I knew we dare not fight, lest we draw Dragon's attention. I looked desperately about for the angel I had seen a moment earlier. "Solon!"

\* \* \*

Rhys was about to dash for the gate when he heard a sound behind him. A large hand grabbed the neck of his tunic and dragged him backward. It pulled him down with amazing

177

strength. His head hit the ground, and, for a moment, the earth seemed to spin above him. Someone the size of a bear knelt over him and grasped tightly at his throat.

"Got lost along the way from the abbey, aye?" the man asked. Rhys gasped for breath as he looked into the fleshy face of Baldric. "Most people enter the manor house through the front. Ah, but I thought you might end up here after your first attempt failed."

Rhys tried to push Baldric away, but the weight and strength of the man were too much for him. "Let me go!" Rhys hissed as loud as he could with Baldric's fingers wrapped around his throat.

"Little chance of that!" Baldric grinned. "Acwellen will be quite pleased to see you. The effect will be greater if I take you while you're still breathing, but dead will work as well."

"Let me go!"

Baldric released his grip on Rhys' neck slightly. "Now then, do you want to go before Acwellen and plead for mercy? Or shall I just choke you here and get it over with?"

Rhys struggled to pull Baldric's hand from his neck. He gasped for air and tried to push himself up with his feet to get Baldric off him.

"That's the way you'll have it, aye? Guess I'll have to carry your body to my lord." Baldric's grip tightened. Just as Rhys began to feel a blackness come over him, a voice came from behind Baldric. "Let'm go."

Baldric loosened his grip and turned to the man, "Nay. He's a criminal, wanted by orders of Lord Acwellen himself."

Rhys could not see the man or tell what was happening; he heard steps, felt Baldric suddenly release his throat, saw Baldric's head snap back as he fell over. A balding man with a gray beard stood over Rhys and Baldric with a large hammer. It was Ormod.

Ormod glanced at Rhys. "Didn't want to argue with'm. Those people from the manor house always want to argue."

Rhys stood up slowly. His legs were weak and his throat hurt, but he bowed slightly to Ormod. "Thank you, sir," he said in a quiet, hoarse voice.

Ormod bent down and placed his ear next to Baldric's mouth while pinching his nose with his fingers. "Don't hear a breath. But don't think I be killin' him with one blow."

The stocky man stood up and peered at Rhys curiously with one eyebrow cocked. "Don't know what you be doing here."

Rhys swallowed and whispered, "Heard Alayn be fighting a thane tomorrow. Thought I might get to him through the gate."

"Aye. Been watchin' that gate me self. But there be no gettin' through now. There be men guardin' the gate on the other side of the hedges." He rubbed his bearded chin and then pointed in the direction of the hedges. "Look there. See that shiny spot? Watchman's sword. Just waitin' for someone to try to sneak through that gate."

Rhys swallowed again. He realized he would have been at the gate by now if Baldric had not caught him. "What'll you do?" he asked.

The smith tapped the handle of his hammer. "Can't let him fight alone. I'll fight with him...die with him, I suppose."

\* \* \*

The devils, having anticipated Rhys' death, were angry. They glared at Solon, Ormod's guardian. As I had hoped, Solon had quickly drawn Ormod's attention in our direction, and Ormod had come to Rhys' defense. Though Ormod had not intended to kill Baldric, the man was dead. And while the devils love to see the innocent slain, they hate to lose one who does their bidding. They gnashed their rotting teeth at us, but they did no more for they did not want to risk angering Dragon by starting a fight.

\* \* \*

To avoid being tracked by Acwellen's hounds, Rhys and Ormod found a stream and waded up it half a mile before

Ormod made his way back to the smith shop and Rhys returned to the hiding place. It was nearly dark when Rhys reached the brothers. He told them all about the encounter with Baldric and Ormod. The story left them wide-eyed and quiet, the only sounds being the chirping of crickets and the croaking of frogs.

"Then Ormod intends to join the battle?" Carlyle asked.

Rhys nodded and said, "There be nothing for us to do then; I suppose, but to go to the contest and stand with him."

"Unless God shows us some other way," Carlyle said.

That night the round harvest moon slipped in and out of the clouds. Somewhere north of Edenton a wolf howled at it. Rhys sat next to the stream, listening to the water babbling over the rocks and staring into the dark.

"Can you not sleep?" asked Carlyle from behind him.

"I had my whole life to sleep. I'll spend the last of it awake."

"A little sleep at the right time refreshes the heart."

"Do you suppose that Alayn be sleeping?"

Carlyle didn't answer.

"I heard the Voice you told me about. The One that speaks to the heart."

"Aye?" Carlyle asked.

"The Voice said that I be Lord Protector of Edenton. Bors tried to be Lord Protector and failed because it wasn't his. I be made for it. I never thought that about anything before. But when the Voice said it, I knew 'twas true." Rhys paused and stared into the darkness. "But then when I saw Ormod today, the Voice seemed unreal, as if it never happened."

"I suppose seeing Ormod reminded you of your days as a smith," Carlyle said.

Rhys nodded.

Moonlight flickered across Carlyle's face. "Not many lords make good smiths. And few smiths make good lords. You were never meant to be a smith. 'Tis folly to judge all of your life by your failure at something you were never meant to do."

"If it's a lord I'll be, then why be it so painful?"

For a moment, Carlyle made no reply. The frogs croaked, and one of the monks started snoring. Finally, Carlyle said, "Resisting evil is never easy, but the struggle is what makes a man strong."

# Chapter 21

## THE CHALLENGE

At dawn, Ormod opened the door to his shop. The darkness in the room lessened, and his eyes adjusted enough to see. He walked across the room to where a sword lay on the workbench. He lifted it. He cut the air with a short stroke and frowned: after swinging a hammer for so many years, the sword felt too light. He laid the sword down and looked about the room. His eyes fell on the battle axe that he had sharpened for one of Acwellen's thanes. Ormod picked up the battle axe and felt its heft. The weight was near the end, like a hammer. Suddenly, he raised the battle axe over his head and brought its full force down on the wooden workbench. The workbench crashed to the floor in a hail of splinters, tongs, and hammers. He gazed at the broken workbench. The battle axe would do.

The room darkened as the light from the doorway was blocked by the figure of a man. Ormod turned to face him and saw there were two monks. The large one nodded at him and stepped through the door. The smaller one had a rook sitting on his shoulder.

"We were told, kind smith, by the young man, Rhys, that you might have some weapons by which we might defend ourselves and our friends today."

By mid-morning, the merchants had finished laying out their goods for the last day of Loafmas There were tables with leather goods, colored fabrics, potions, ales, and wines. Edenton's farmers and craftsmen, as well as servants from the manor walked among the displays. Some of those at the feast had returned to their homes in nearby villages. But new visitors arrived for the final day to buy, eat, and watch the contest. And, in the midst of the bustle, the people noticed an odd site—monks, in three groups of twos, arriving at the festival carrying quarter staffs, and, in a few cases, a sword or battle axe.

\* \* \*

Angels stood in groups, whispering to one another and glancing at us. Many fingered their sword hilts as if they guessed that the long period of truce was about to end. The devils, however, were drunk with the anticipation of an innocent man's death. It was the kind of evil that clouded their souls with frenzied delight.

"There are two of them to each one of us," Zophar said quietly to those in our small band.

Haelstrum nodded at Rhys. "It all depends on what our man believes in his heart. This battle will be won or lost there."

\* \* \*

Lord Acwellen's servants worked on the lawn in front of the manor house, setting chairs on the wooden platform on which Acwellen and his family would sit and roping off the area for the contest. The reeve climbed up on the platform to review the preparations. He stared out across the rapidly growing crowd. He had expected a large crowd for the contest. But he was startled at the sight of half a dozen monks, tonsured and black-robed, standing among the villagers. He knew Benedictine monks; they abhorred this sort of contest. When he saw another monk with a quarter staff in his hands, he swore and barked, "Hunlaf!"

A bearded thane with shaggy hair climbed the stairs to the platform. "Here I be, sir."

The reeve climbed down the stairs with the thane following him. "There are monks here in the crowd. I don't know why, but I'll be telling Lord Acwellen. Bring the prisoners round. And check on our man. Make sure he'll be armed and ready to go in half an hour. Tell him not to end it too quickly, got to give the crowd what they come for. Now, go!"

The thane grunted a reply and walked quickly toward the buildings behind the manor house. The reeve entered the side door to the manor house mumbling to himself, "Monks. The devil take them. What be they up to?"

Inside he found grey-bearded Lord Acwellen dressed in a red tunic and a cape sitting in his great hall chair. Crosnan paced beside him, frowning.

"Is everything ready?" Lord Acwellen asked.

The reeve bowed, "Aye, my lord. But there be one thing. There be at least half a dozen Benedictine monks out there."

"Monks? Where?"

"In the crowd, gathered around the ropes for the contest."

Crosnan laughed. "Should the holy among us not have a little fun also? Cedric, you worry more than an old woman! Are you afraid of a monk?"

"Not I. But I want to know what they are doing here. Monks don't approve of these contests. So why be they here?"

Acwellen raised his hands for silence. "They tried to free the prisoner once. Perhaps they want to try again. Who can tell? Tell your men this, Cedric, if the monks try something, slaughter them all. Just not the villagers. We need them for the harvest. Now, get the prisoners, and let us get this contest started."

The reeve bowed and left the manor house to retrieve the prisoners.

Rhys moved through the crowd holding his bow next to his body so it couldn't get broken. A gray-haired woman saw him and gave a little gasp. She turned to the man next to her and began whispering. Others looked and whispered to their neighbors. "Be that the smith's other son?" they asked. "The one everyone said be dead?"

"Where did these monks come from?" others murmured.

When the other monks saw Carlyle and Rhys, they moved through the crowd toward them. The Edenton villagers moved aside till Rhys and the monks formed a small knot on the edge of the roped contest field.

Rhys and the brothers watched as the thanes gathered around the platform holding shields and swords ready as if to defend the platform from attack. "Looks as if they fear the crowd," Carlyle told Rhys. Two of the thanes came around the right side of the platform leading Bors with his hands tied in front of him. A murmur went through the brothers when they saw Bors. To the left of the platform, two thanes led a young man. "Is that Alayn?" Carlyle asked. Rhys nodded, staring at the oddly thin figure. Behind the thanes, Rhys could see the long red hair of Aethaelwynn. She held her hands in front of her mouth with her palms together, as if she were praying.

\* \* \*

The angels gathered on the lawn in front of the brothers. Across the way where Acwellen sat were mostly devils, though some angels were scattered about with their charges. The tension grew like Nuriel's storm clouds. Lord Acwellen, and Lady Gwendolyn mounted the wooden platform. Behind them stood the awful, mighty Dragon. His eyes burned like coals, and he gave a foul odor. He flapped his black wings and roared, fire spewing from his mouth.

The devils gathered around Dragon. Flying devils darkened the sky like vultures ready to descend on the dead. Their wings beat the air and spread their foul smell. The devils that did not fly beat their spears and axes on the ground, working themselves into a frenzy. They screamed dark incantations we could not understand and would not have uttered if we had.

Suddenly Dragon saw me. He shouted, "What are you doing here, Guardian of Edenton?!" The cries of the devils lessened to a murmur while Dragon whipped his tail and worked his talons in anger. "Are you come to destroy me?" he growled.

I shouted above the noise of the devils, "We must watch over our charges!"

Dragon's gaze shifted to the monks. He whipped his tail within a few feet of the brothers. "Then it is they that have come to destroy me!" With that he lifted his front talon and reached for Rhys. I had only an instant to act. I drew my sword and, dashing forward, aimed a blow at Dragon. My sword glanced off a talon as if I had struck the side of a rock. Dragon whipped his head around breathing fire across the manor house lawn. The shouting and frenzy stopped. All eyes turned to Dragon. I raised my sword as a means of shielding myself. For a moment he eyed me as a hawk looks upon its prey. Then the gates of hell flew open. Devils charged across the lawn and fell on us from the sky. Dragon snatched me up with his talons and held me in the air.

* * *

Rhys felt his face burning even though the sun was behind thick clouds. Fear took him like a wave upon the shore, and it was as if all hell waged war in his bowels. He struggled to breathe. He glanced at Carlyle for assurance and saw him mouthing the words to a prayer.

Suddenly the reeve stood on the platform. "Friends," he shouted in his odd, high-pitched voice. He looked at the monks and hesitated before adding, "and visitors, at the finale of the May Day fair we brought you a battle that was of great interest and entertainment. Now, on the last day of the Festival of Loafmas, Lord Acwellen has agreed to allow another challenge…."

*Now!* urged the voice inside of Rhys. His heart beat against his chest. Whatever he would do, he must do it now. The monks waited. Carlyle held his breath and prayed. The anxious voices in Rhys' head stilled and a single word formed: *challenge*. The reeve's word, *challenge*, echoed inside of Rhys. His mind cleared, and he knew what he must do. He reached for the rope in front of him, stepped over it, and walked out onto the field.

The reeve stopped in the middle of his announcement. He stared at the young man standing on the contest field. A murmur swept through the crowd. Alayn saw Rhys through weak eyes and felt confused. Aethaelwynn held her breath and prayed.

* * *

Dragon turned from me and stared at Rhys with a mixture of fascination and dread. Relaxing his talons, he let me slip free. The fighting all around me stopped as the devils and angels turned to see what was happening. Rhys stood alone in the middle of the roped contest field. He had no sign of great strength to cause fear in Dragon. He simply carried a bow and a quiver of arrows. But Dragon sensed the same spirit was with him that accompanied the Christ when He entered the gates of hell—unflinching courage in the face of overwhelming evil.

* * *

"You!" the reeve shouted. "Get off the contest field! Only those who have made the challenge may stand on the field."

"I'll not leave the field. I am here to issue the challenge!"

Crosnan leaned over to Acwellen and whispered, "'Tis the brother of that poacher, Alayn. This is the very one we have been looking for!"

"You cannot issue a challenge!" the reeve cried out in his squeaky voice. "The Lord of Edenton has already approved a challenge!"

"I am the son of Lord Erlan and the true Lord of Edenton. Acwellen murdered my father and stole the lordship from him!" Rhys shouted.

The villagers gasped in disbelief. Though Acwellen's means of becoming the lord of Edenton was well known, it was not spoken of publicly. Surely, they thought, Acwellen would have the young man hanged for treason.

The reeve turned to the thanes standing by the platform. "Arrest him!" he ordered.

Three of the thanes started toward Rhys. As they did, Ormod raised his battle axe and stepped between them and Rhys. Another villager stepped forward with a spear and another with a hay fork. Carlyle and the monks took their weapons in their hands and, pushing down the rope, moved forward several steps onto the contest field. The reeve motioned for all the thanes toward the field. "Arrest them," he shouted. "If they resist, kill them!"

Another murmur went through the crowd and several more men stepped forward with spears. At the sight of the village men coming out, the thanes stopped and looked toward the reeve. The reeve frowned and looked at Acwellen for orders.

Acwellen jumped to his feet, angry that the defiance of the villagers and monks had tested the mettle of his thanes so quickly. But Crosnan whispered in his father's ear, "No doubt the thanes can beat them, but we may have nothing to eat next year when there is no one to harvest. Let me bargain with this rebellious boy."

Acwellen looked firmly at his son. "So long as none of those monks live," he swore. Crosnan nodded and stepped next to the reeve. "What challenge do you propose?" he shouted to Rhys.

"One arrow at a target from fifty paces. The closest to the center of the target wins."

"And what terms do you propose?" Crosnan asked.

"If I win," Rhys said, "Acwellen must return the lordship to me peacefully."

Crosnan smiled. "If we win, you and all those with you hang for the charge of treason."

"Nay. If you win, Acwellen gets to keep what he stole.

Nothing more. And you must release Alayn and the prisoner, Bors."

Crosnan laughed and shook his head. "Why should my lord try to win what is already his? But for the sake of the entertainment, we will compromise. If we win, we exchange Alayn for you. Agreed?"

"What about Bors?" Rhys asked.

Crosnan frowned. "Do not press my lord's patience with your demands, boy! Are we agreed?"

Rhys realized that Acwellen's patience would not last long. And, if he did not win, none of his terms would be met anyway.

"Aye," he said.

Acwellen instructed the reeve to bring forth a target for the contest. He handed Crosnan a hunting knife and said, "If you lose this contest, kill the young man with the bow. I will take care of the smith's son. The reeve and the thanes will kill the rest." Crosnan nodded and slipped the hunting knife into his belt.

Rhys walked back to the brothers. He stared down at his hands. "I can't stop them from shaking," he said.

Carlyle took Rhys' left hand in his right and made the sign of the cross. Rhys held both hands out—the left one was as steady as a ship in harbor, but the right one continued to shake.

"Do the other hand," Carlyle said.

Rhys stared at him as if he didn't understand. Carlyle took Rhys' right hand and made the sign of the cross with it. Rhys gazed at his unshaking hands.

Carlyle looked sternly at Rhys. "Listen to me," he said. "One arrow will not be enough. As soon as you hit the target, put another arrow to the string. Do you understand?"

Rhys looked blankly at him. "Do you understand?" Carlyle demanded.

Rhys nodded. He looked down at his hands, took a deep breath, and walked back on to the contest field.

Herlwin prayed, "Our Father which art in heaven…"

The reeve brought out a target that looked like a wooden door with rings painted on it. It was placed on the contest field to the left side of the platform. The reeve stepped off fifty paces and marked the spot from which they would launch their arrows. Then he announced with a squeaky shout, "Crosnan will represent the lordship. He will go first. The challenger will go last."

\* \* \*

Dragon seemed to have lost interest in the battle that raged mere moments previous. He stared at Rhys while devils and angels stood holding their weapons, knowing that this was the moment Edenton's fate would be decided.

# Chapter 22

## THE ARROW

Carrying a bow and quiver, Crosnan stepped to the line, selected an arrow from the quiver, and placed it on the string. He raised the bow and pulled the string back to his cheek. Seconds passed as he sighted along the arrow. Edenton watched in silence. Crosnan released the string. The arrow shot through the air and struck the target. The people on the platform and the thanes cheered. The arrow was on the very edge of the small red circle in the center of the target. Crosnan smiled and bowed to the people on the platform before eyeing Rhys with a look of disgust borne from years of indulgence. "The lordship is mine. No smithing boy will take it from me," Crosnan said loud enough for only Rhys to hear.

*He knows nothing of me,* Rhys thought, *or of Ormod, or Carlyle, or even of my hands—how still they be.* He looked past Crosnan and saw Ormod holding his battle axe next to the gray-headed miller. He saw the monks in their black robes standing as free as any men on earth. And then, there was the target with its red ring. Everything else faded and in all the world there was only Rhys and the target—the red ring on the target.

Only one place on the target could Rhys put his arrow to beat Crosnan. His arrow would have to be just to the right of Crosnan's arrow, anywhere else and Rhys would lose. He took a deep breath, selected his arrow, and placed it on the string. Rhys pulled the arrow next to his cheek and held it tight. He estimated the amount the arrow would drop over the distance and raised his aim slightly. He concentrated on the place where his arrow must go, held his breath, counted to three and released the arrow. It leaped from the string like a hound after a hare. For a moment all of heaven and earth stood still. The arrow seemed to hang like a hawk riding the wind; the fate of Edenton riding with it. Then the arrow found the target and split the wood with a "thwack." A moment of stunned silence passed before a cheer erupted from the brothers and the villagers. Rhys' arrow was in the very center of the red ring.

As Rhys stared at the arrow, everything around him seemed to begin moving at once. The reeve stepped forward and pulled Rhys' arrow out of the target. "I declare Lord Acwellen the winner!" he screeched. A roar of protest arose. The reeve turned to the thanes and motioned them to advance on the monks.

Rhys suddenly remembered what Carlyle had said—he would need more than one arrow. But as he reached for another arrow, he saw someone coming at him from his left side. Rhys turned as Crosnan lunged at him with a knife. Rhys spun away just as Crosnan's knife cut the air next to his ear. Rhys lost his balance and landed on his knees. He looked over his shoulder and saw Crosnan turning to come at him again. Then Herlwin appeared from behind. Crosnan heard the approach and looked around. Herlwin swung his quarter staff at Crosnan's head, dropping him like a bag of onions. Herlwin's eyes met Rhys, and Rhys saw the fierce and wild gaze of a warrior. He wished for Herlwin's simple grin, but feared it was lost forever.

The reeve and Acwellen's thanes were coming at them. Already the miller was down, and Ormod was swinging his axe as several thanes came at him. The brothers ran to Ormod's aid, where one was cut down. The thanes would have quickly overwhelmed the brothers and villagers had the one guarding

Bors not turned his back on the prisoner. Bors stood so quietly during the commotion that the thane forgot about him for a moment and turned to watch the fight. In an instant, Bors wrapped the rope binding his hands around the thane's throat and choked the man till his legs went limp, and he fell to the ground. Though Bors' hands were still tied, he took the thane's sword and dashed across the contest field to join the battle. One of the thanes turned just as Bors reached him, but Bors dropped him with the cut of his sword. The reeve and another thane turned to fight Bors.

The world around Rhys fell into madness—women screaming, men shouting and striking at one another, people running every which way. But the confusion lifted from Rhys' mind when he saw Bors struggling against the reeve and the thane. Rhys remembered the arrow he had on the string. He brought up the bow, realizing that this time he wasn't aiming at a deer, but a man. *Yes*, he thought, *but this man is trying to kill Bors*. The thane lifted his sword to bring it down on Bors when Rhys released the arrow. It hit the thane's exposed side and put the man on the ground gasping for air.

\* \* \*

We fought the devils as they poured down upon us. Dunstan's guardian went down, just as Dunstan did. Ormod and his guardian, Solon, fell. We were close to being overwhelmed, and Dragon had not yet joined the attack. Eleazar slowed the devils by attacking their flank. But they were slowed only momentarily. Carlyle was down, and Haelstrum disappeared in a sea of devils. I realized that in only a few more seconds we would be completely overrun—Rhys and the brothers would be dead and our mission ended in failure. Dragon turned toward Alayn, who stood near to it, and crouched like a cat preparing to pounce.

\* \* \*

Rhys put another arrow on the string when a tall man he had never seen before grabbed his arm. "There!" the man shouted, pointing toward the platform.

Rhys looked and saw Acwellen striding toward Alayn with a hunting knife. Alayn's hands were still tied behind him, and Aethaelwynn stood in front of him trying to shield him from Acwellen. Rhys could barely hear Aethaelwynn's screams above the shouting and clashing of weapons. Rhys started running toward the platform, but stopped when he saw Acwellen push Aethaelwynn aside.

"Acwellen!" Rhys shouted. The battle din lessened for a moment as thanes turned to see what was happening. Acwellen eyed Rhys with contempt before turning his back on him. Rhys focused on the spot of Acwellen's back between the shoulder blades. He brought the bow up, pulled back the string, held his breath and released the string—while never losing focus on the spot. The arrow caught Acwellen with his hand and knife in the air. It pitched him forward, and he fell on Alayn. The cries of battle went silent. Everyone stood staring at the two bodies lying on the ground in front of the platform. Aethaelwynn stepped forward and rolled Acwellen off of Alayn. Alayn got to his knees, but Acwellen lay still.

"He be dead!" Aethaelwynn shouted.

\* \* \*

Just as the giant beast reached for Alayn, Rhys' arrow pierced the heart of Acwellen, and he breathed his last. Dragon wrenched and screamed in agony. He had made himself strong through Acwellen and now the brutish man was gone.

At Dragon's cry, devils and angels across the field of battle turned to see what had happened. Dragon, which had ruled the devils through fear of his strength, lay panting on the ground like a wounded dog. The devils' fear of Dragon faded quickly. It was the angels that they feared now, for the angels could send them to hell. The devils began to run or fly from the battle, and Dragon was helpless to stop them.

\* \* \*

The brothers and villagers gripped their weapons expecting the battle to begin again, but it did not. The thanes looked around them—Acwellen was dead; Bors had bested the reeve who appeared dead, and Crosnan lie unconscious in the middle of the contest field. There was no one to lead them or punish them if they did not fight. One by one they lay down their weapons and bowed their knees in loyalty to Rhys.

Rhys gazed about the manor house lawn. The violence had swept across it like a thunderstorm. There were little rings of people around bloodied bodies. Women wept for their husbands, and there were cries for help for the wounded. Rhys saw Leof bending over Carlyle. He ran past the kneeling thanes and knelt next to Leof to see Carlyle's ashen face and bloody chest.

"Be he dead?" Rhys asked.

Leof shook his head. "He's losing blood. Can we get the wounded inside somewhere?"

"We'll have to use the manor house," Rhys said.

Ormod had blood on his chest and hands, but was trying to get up. Rhys helped him hold his head up. "I'll be goin' to see Alayn's mother soon," he whispered. "I be sorry, Rhys. I didn't know how to father a lord."

"Don't be sorry, sir. You saved me more than once—Alayn and I both owe our lives to you."

"I be glad for that," Ormod said with much effort. "Did you see Alayn? Be he alright?"

"Here, Father."

Alayn knelt down on the other side of Ormod and took his head in his hands. Someone pulled at Rhys' shoulder, and Rhys stood to see Bors. Bors leaned close to him. "We be in a tricksy spot here, Rhys. At any moment, one of these thanes could take up his sword and lead the rest in killing us all. When Crosnan comes to, they'll have a leader. It be a harsh thing to say, but the wise thing to do would be to kill them. Otherwise, they may undo it all, and all that have died may have died for nothing."

Rhys felt as if he was in a thick fog and things were happening around him that he could not grasp. He knew Bors was talking about Acwellen's thanes, but he could not believe that Bors meant "kill" them like he would kill a deer. Rhys saw Alayn weeping over Ormod and he thought, *Ormod's dead. Carlyle may be soon.* Bors said something that Rhys didn't understand; he walked over to a kneeling thane and raised his sword over him. The man cowered in fear, and Rhys suddenly understood what was happening.

"Nay!" Rhys shouted. He ran to the thane and picked up the sword lying in front of him. He raised the sword and faced Bors with it. "Nay!" he cried again. "He laid down his sword!"

Bors stared at the angry young man facing him and realized there was something in Rhys that he had lost long ago. Bors lowered the sword slowly and said haltingly, "Aye…Rhys…aye. We'll just gather up the swords."

The eye of every thane was on Rhys. He felt himself shaking from the inside out. He couldn't stop it. The sword he held in the air shook till he drove it into the ground to steady himself. His legs felt weak enough to buckle. He realized what Bors had said was true—any moment one thane could take up his sword and lead the rest against them. But something interrupted his thoughts, something that sounded powerful. It sounded like thunder, but not quite; more like something pounding the earth. He turned, they all turned, and looked down the road that led from Iconium to Edenton; horses, riders with blue and gold banners, a lord and his thanes wearing colors he had never seen before. In the front rode the lord with a beautiful lion-crested shield, finely dressed and riding a splendidly outfitted horse. Next to him rode another who was finely dressed, but with long black hair streaming out behind her.

The horses slowed as the lord and lady gazed at the odd battlefield before them. Then Elene saw Rhys and Bors and pointed in their direction. They spurred their horses and rode across the manor house lawn to where the two men stood before the kneeling thane. They stared at the scene before them as the winded, sweaty horses stamped the ground and shook their heads.

Elene said, "We heard about the abbey and that you were arrested, Bors, and we were afraid that Acwellen...we were afraid you would be dead."

"I be alive now only cause of Rhys and the brothers and villagers. Rhys killed Acwellen."

The steely eyes of Lord Eadmund grew a little larger. "Acwellen is dead?" he asked Rhys.

"Aye," Rhys said, still holding the sword to steady himself. "And there are wounded that need tended to."

Lord Eadmund turned to the man behind him. "Take the wounded into the manor house and see that the brothers have everything they need to treat them."

"Where is Crosnan?" Elene asked.

Bors pointed to the young man stirring in the yard, "Herlwin dropped him with a quarterstaff."

"And what of Lady Gwendolyn?" Elene asked.

Elene's question caused Rhys to turn and look at the woman weeping over Acwellen's body. He had given no thought to the fact that Acwellen's wife, and the aunt of he and Elene would be there. Lord Eadmund said to the man who sat on the horse behind him, "Keep the young man and woman under guard till I give you further orders. Gather up all the weapons of Acwellen's thanes and quarter the men in the stables for now."

"Aye, my lord."

"Rhys," Lord Eadmund continued, "When things are put in order and we have eaten, we shall hear from you and Bors what has happened here. Then we shall sign a witness that you are the son of Lord Erlan and are rightly the lord protector of Edenton."

Rhys had not the strength to stand. Still gripping the sword, he lowered himself to one knee and bowed his head.

* * *

With Lord Eadmund's contingent came dozens of angels along with a few trailing devils. And they saw before them devils fleeing like frightened rats. The fight was over, save for a few momentary clashes of swords here and there. Dragon crawled behind the manor house and disappeared. I turned my attention to the wounded angels and men, Haelstrum and Mycynn among them.

As we sorted out who would take the wounded to Orion, a faded angel approached me and bowed. "I understand you have been the leader of this… um…freeing of Edenton."

I nodded.

"I am Uzziel. I've served at the manor house for only a few weeks, but I am at your service."

"Very well," I said. "Look to your charge."

"Ah, but my charge is dead."

"Can you take one of the wounded angels to Orion?"

He shook his head, "I've not the strength for traveling."

"Well, then, if I find something for you to do, I'll have to let you know."

Uzziel nodded at me and gave a sort of odd smile. Something seemed strange about the angel, but we were all weary and there were wounded to attend to, so I gave it little thought.

# Chapter 23

## NEW EDENTON

Carlyle's soul lingered near his feverish body for several days in a dream-like state between the living and the dead. At times he saw us and slept peacefully in our shadows. At other times he would glimpse a devil and become agitated or cry out.

Leof cared for the wounded with poultices and herbs, while Herlwin talked to them, to God, and to anyone else who would listen. Ten had died from the battle, including Dunstan, Guthram, Ormod and two other villagers. Acwellen, the reeve, and three thanes also died. The men were buried and mourned.

Meanwhile, the immense weight of lordship settled quickly on Rhys as he talked long with Lord Eadmund and Elene about what should be done. The thanes who were of good name with the villagers were allowed to stay as long as they did not take up the sword and worked hard in the fields or at a craft; the rest were banned from Edenton. With Ebert and Aethaelwynn's help they decided which servants could stay and which were banned along with the steward.

As nearly a week passed, the duties of lordship became unbearable for Rhys. The manor servants constantly asked for his judgment in matters he knew nothing about—they were not used to making such decisions on their own. Lord Eadmund wanted to talk with him about laws and ordinances that Rhys did not understand. Elene pressed him to force Lady Gwendolyn on the whereabouts of their mother as well as to make changes to the manor house and himself, while Crosnan shouted curses at him from the keep. Added to all of this, Bors, having felt the humiliation of the handling of Acwellen's thanes, would not talk to him. And Carlyle was near death.

At a moment when the manor house was silent, Rhys took his bow and arrows and quietly left the manor house. He took the back gate near the keep. Staying in the trees, he walked round Edenton to the part of the forest where he and Alayn had hunted earlier that summer.

I roused myself from sitting next to the fading fire in the center of the manor house to go with Rhys. But the angel Uzziel stepped forward from the shadows of the manor house and raised his hand. "Do not stir yourself. I will take this watch. There is not else I can do in return for you." Uzziel grinned and made a half bow. I nodded in return. I was not comfortable letting an angel I hardly knew take over my charge, but I wondered, *What could happen? Dragon has been defeated.*

So I settled down next to the fire and stared at the flames licking away at the glowing logs that spit sparks out onto the floor. I wondered what would happen to Carlyle, and I thought again of Bittenrood—wondered if he had been there during the battle and where he was now. Though my own heart was heavy, I heard laughter coming from the manor house lawn. Without Acwellen, Crosnan, or the steward lording themselves over the manor house servants, the younger of them had stolen out onto the manor house lawn to play games. Having lived with oppression all their lives, they tested their new freedoms somewhat carefully, not wanting to risk a flogging if Rhys or Lord Eadmund changed their good natures as lords often did.

My thoughts were interrupted by the opening of the front door. Someone came into the hall whistling, not so much a tune, but just whistling for the sake of it. It was Ebert, perhaps the happiest of the lot. He felt certain that life at the manor had changed for good and knew that it was partly to his credit; after all, he was the one who had sought out Rhys to deliver the message from Aethaelwynn. Afriel, Ebert's guardian, entered the hall and greeted me with a nod and a smile.

Still whistling, Ebert laid a chunk of wood on the fire and stirred the embers with the poker. "The boy's heart is forever merry," I remarked to Afriel.

"Light as the sparrow's feather," he agreed, smiling. "But what of Rhys? The weight of Edenton has been thrust on his shoulders, methinks."

"He's like Atlas of the Greeks, feeling the weight of the world. He went hunting a bit ago—in pursuit of peace as much as a deer, I suspect."

"You didn't go with him?"

I shook my head. "Uzziel has been asking for something to do and offered to go."

Afriel looked confused. "Uzziel?"

"A guardian who came to Edenton not that long ago. His charge was killed in the battle."

"I know all the men who were killed in the battle and their guardians," Afriel said, "save for...Acwellen."

Uzziel's strange introduction immediately after the battle troubled me all along, but I had ignored it. Dragons can change shapes, assume other identities, as well as angels can. Uzziel did not seem especially powerful, but the Dragon was weakened by Acwellen's death. And now I realized that, because of my carelessness, Dragon, disguised as Uzziel, was this very moment alone with Rhys.

I leapt to my feet, knocking over a chunk of wood which scared the wits out of Ebert.

"This is it, then!" I shouted, drawing my sword. "Dragon and I will have it out now!"

"I'll go with you," Afriel cried.

"No. I want word sent to Orion to get Haelstrum and Zophar back here now. I want this manor house and this town cleared of every devil that sneaks about with no charges to guard. Clear every alley way, every cottage!"

I started out the back of the manor house, but realized that Rhys had just gone that way to not be seen. He would have gone around Edenton to hunt near the stream that he was familiar with. I ran across the front lawn, where the servants shivered from the sudden breeze, past cottages and the smith shop. I ran across the golden meadow to where the shadows of the trees led to the forest. I slowed, walking quickly but quietly along the stream to the path where earlier this summer Rhys had attempted to shoot what he thought was a stag. *He has to be here...somewhere,* I thought. *If he is hunting, he would be here; this is the place he knows and hunts. Why would he not be hunting? What else? What would Dragon try to get him to do? Take his life?* I didn't think he was desperate enough for that. *Run away?* I turned toward the road to Iconium and started running. I had not gone far, when the trees seemed to begin to sway about me. A discordant sound came to me, tearing at my soul and making me want to weep. I struggled to think or breathe. I stopped to steady myself when I saw Rhys thirty yards in front of me, stooped over and trudging away from Edenton. Dragon, in the form of Uzziel, whispered in his ear, "Carlyle's dead. You're all alone. That proud Bors and his self-serving ways, he wants it all for himself. And Lord Eadmund, who does he think he is telling you what to do? He just showed up when the battle was over...."

"Dragon!"

He turned to me. His face now looked like that of a serpent. A forked tongue flicked out of his mouth. "Go back to your village," he hissed. "He's mine now, and he'll have nothing to do with your noble lordship."

"I'm going back," I shouted, "and he's going with me." I ran at the beast with all the strength I had while the world seemed to tilt, and Dragon stared unblinking at me. The screams of all the devils in hell sounded in my soul. I shouted to drown out the noise and raised my sword above my head.

Dragon faced me with his sword raised. I drew back my sword and swung at him. He blocked my stroke and stepped enough to the side to allow my momentum to carry me past him. I fell, rolled over, and came up on my feet, bringing my sword up just in time to block Dragon's stroke. But the power behind Dragon's stroke was greater than any I had ever felt before. It knocked me backwards and out of Dragon's reach. He came at me again, his eyes unblinking and tongue flicking. Again, I blocked his stroke and was knocked backwards. The third time he came at me, I saw the stroke was coming from the side, so I ducked under it and came up with a swing at Dragon's shoulder. My sword missed, just grazing the edge of Dragon's garment. Again and again Dragon knocked me backwards with his powerful strokes. I realized that Dragon was too powerful for me, so I tried to keep moving away from Rhys, hoping that he would somehow free himself from the thoughts Dragon had planted.

I got up from another blow not knowing how many more I could withstand. My sword felt as heavy as a tree. I backed away from Dragon again, but as he came at me I heard a sound—a song like those sung at the throne of heaven. The voices were those of angels, and the song was one I had never heard before, yet I knew the words before they were sung. I began to sing the song; it took no strength, and in truth the singing seemed to give me new strength.

The song implored the Creator's kingdom come and His will be done on earth as it is in the heavens. My singing infuriated Dragon, and his stroke again knocked me to the ground. But I got up quickly and continued singing the song, how the Lord of all Lords would return to the earth and every king would lay his kingdom at the Lord's feet....

Clang! Dragon struck, and I staggered backward but stayed on my feet. I continued the song, how every tribe and nation on the earth would bow their knee to the Lord. And He would rule the earth with mercy, justice, and kindness....

Clang! He struck again, but this time I held my ground. Dragon's strength seemed to flow out of him like the tide of the sea. I could sense his anger turning to desperation. But I sang on, how every enemy would be defeated and the Christ would offer His Father, all power and glory and honor....

Dragon blinked and hissed, "Stop."

That heavenly song ended, so I stopped singing. And as I did, all the devastation Dragon had brought about—from the beginning at Erlan's death, to the battle in Edenton, and this present treachery, burned through me like a fiery arrow. I forgot my weariness. With the zeal of the Lord, I raised my sword and brought it down on Dragon. He blocked my sword, but I brought the sword down on him again. Dragon blocked my strokes but began to fall back. I brought the sword down for Rhys' loss of his father, for Ormod's drunkenness, for Alayn's imprisonment, and for Ebert's scars. My final blow knocked the sword from his hands, and he stood glaring at me with oily eyes.

"This is the second time you have been defeated in this cause," I said. "Leave your sword, and flee this place, lest you find yourself in hell."

Dragon glanced at Rhys. I stepped forward, raised my sword, ready to aim a blow at Dragon's head. But he stepped back, then turned and began to run away from Edenton.

Rhys was a hundred yards away and heading north.

A moment later, I stood before Rhys, appearing as the largest man he had ever seen. I was twice his size, a Goliath to him, with flowing white hair. Rhys gasped and stepped back. He reached for his bow and pulled an arrow from the quiver.

"You'll not need that," I said in a voice that sounded to him like thunder. "Where are you going?"

At the sound of my voice, Rhys' knees buckled, and he fell face down in front of me. I waited for a moment, but he appeared lifeless. "Get up," I said.

Several minutes went by before Rhys slowly pushed himself up and stood.

"I asked you where you are going."

He stared at me as if he were seeing a ghost. "To the sea, I guess."

"Are you not the Lord Protector of Edenton?"

"For a few days."

"A few days?"

"'Tis more than I can do. Everyone wants something from me. I was raised by a smith, not a lord."

"You thought it would be easier?"

"It be too hard. The servants want orders, Lord Eadmund wants laws, Elene wants me to be my father, and Carlyle be on his death bed."

"Nothing you were created to do is too hard. It is just hard enough."

Rhys sank to one knee before me. "Are you the risen Lord?"

I took hold of his shoulder and pulled him to his feet.

"No. My name is Iothiel. I was sent to help you free Edenton from Acwellen and Dragon."

"Sent to help me?" Rhys cried. "I've had no one helping me. I've been alone, and I've not seen you before."

"You've never been alone. I was with you when the midwife took you to Ormod. I was the stag you chased into the wood when Alayn was arrested. I was with you when you and Carlyle and Herlwin went to the manor house and when the Grim worshippers gave you the deer. And I was the one who directed you to use your arrow on Acwellen. But had you been able to see me, you would not have needed faith."

Rhys swayed back on his feet, and I caught his shoulder again, this time to steady him. "What sort of man be you?" he asked.

"I am no man. And I only stand before you now because you have listened to the lies of a devil, and it has robbed you of hope."

"Hope? In what?"

"That the Lord and His servants will never leave you—though times may be hard. That you can do whatever the Lord asks of you. And I have been told that your father, Lord Erlan, has seen what you have done and is pleased."

"What to do you mean, 'My father has seen me?' Where could he be?"

"He's in the heavens."

Rhys wiped his face with his sleeve and stared at the ground for a few minutes before looking at me with shining eyes. "Will Carlyle live? I need someone…a man I can see…to help me."

"That decision is not mine, but I will do everything I can to see that he lives long enough to help you."

"Since you know that I was raised by Ormod," he said, "you know in truth that I know not what to do."

"Go back to Edenton and rule over it. Rule justly but with kindness and mercy; and as for truth—cling to it. The voice of the Lord only speaks truth. Lies are the devils' trade. Do not listen to them."

Rhys dropped his gaze and took a deep breath at the sting in my exhortation. But his faith had begun to take root. "Will you go with me?" he asked.

"Only a short way in this visible body. It is against our nature and our calling to attract attention to ourselves. That's how the first angel got into trouble."

Rhys looked at the way ahead of him: toward Iconium and, to the west of that, the sea. He took a deep breath, lifted his head, and turned toward Edenton. As we walked toward the village, he glanced at me, and then to the way ahead. He started to ask a question, when I interrupted his thought.

"Remember this, Rhys—when we took you to Ormod to raise, we did the best we could at the moment. It was not such a bad beginning."

He frowned and nodded.

"Never use it to hide from what you are called to. You may not have learned the things a lord usually is taught, but you learned the difference between good and evil, and nothing is more important than that."

"Yes, sir," Rhys said quietly. But when he turned to look at me, he could not see me.

When we reached the edge of Edenton, Herlwin came running toward Rhys shouting, "There you are! Come! The testimony for your lordship is at hand!"

Hermes flew about Herlwin's head as the monk pointed toward the manor house. "They're gathering on the lawn!

We've been looking all over for you!"

Rhys stopped. I whispered in his ear, "Go on." He looked around for me, but realized I could not be seen. Slowly he began walking toward Edenton, but he quickened his pace as Herlwin shouted and waved his arms in the air like a tree in a storm.

There was music—pipes and drums playing—and torches set around the lawn to ward off the evening gloom. Men returning from the wheat harvest were in a light-hearted mood, for it was rumored that Lord Rhys would let them keep a greater portion of their harvest than Acwellen did. The lightness of the evening and the sound of the pipes caused young women to begin dancing. Before long, young men from the wheat harvest began to join in. Aethaelwynn pulled Alayn into the line of dancers. Alayn, though thin from his months in the keep, almost looked healthy again. Ebert jumped in and, as he spun through the line, waved at Rhys.

From the manor house came Lord Eadmund, Elene, and a brother who had come with them to Edenton. They waited for a moment, allowing the dancing to continue. Then Lord Eadmund raised his hands and the music came to a stop. The dancers, laughing and breathless, turned to Lord Eadmund.

"We are here today..." Lord Eadmund shouted over the crowd, then paused, waiting for them to quiet down. "We gather here this eve to bear witness to the lordship of Rhys, son of Lord Erlan...."

The people cheered. There were shouts of "Long live Lord Rhys!" And the noise went on till Lord Eadmund raised his hands again.

"Let it be recognized that all here today affirm that Lord Erlan was the rightful lord of Edenton seventeen years hence."

Next to Lord Eadmund sat the brother with a large parchment and a quill pen. He scribbled Lord Eadmund's words on the parchment.

"Be it so affirmed?" Eadmund asked.

"Aye!" shouted the people.

"Let it be recognized that Acwellen, through treachery, caused Lord Erlan to be killed and stole the lordship for himself. Be it so affirmed?"

"Aye!"

"Be there any further testimony on this matter?"

The rows of people parted and a large man moved forward. It was Bors. The crowd became silent. Many of the older ones remembered that Bors was an eyewitness to Acwellen's treachery.

"Lord Erlan be my very best friend," he paused to wipe his sleeve across his face. "I saw him die at Acwellen's hands, and I be seeing it every day hence. Some time back I found this fair man in a cave, hiding from Acwellen. I saw then that he be the very image of Lord Erlan. And now, as be fitting, he be Lord Rhys, and all things be made right."

Bors wiped his face again and then made his way through the villagers to where Rhys stood. He hugged Rhys, before disappearing into the crowd.

Lord Eadmund looked down at the scribe to make sure Bors' testimony had been recorded.

The red-haired Aethaelwynn stepped forward and said, "Alayn be too ashamed to say it, but after Lord Rhys tried to rescue him he told me that Ormod, God rest his soul, said that Rhys be the son of Lord Erlan. The mid-wife brought Rhys to his house the night Lord Erlan be killed. Ormod never told Rhys, because he didn't want him to think he be better than a smith."

Rhys blinked and looked at Alayn. Their eyes met briefly before Alayn looked away.

"Need we any more testimony?" Lord Eadmund shouted.

The men and women shook their heads and a few shouted, "Nay!"

"Then by rights of birth, Rhys, being the only son of Lord Erlan, is the rightful Lord of Edenton. Be it so affirmed?"

"Aye!" the people shouted and another cheer went up.

Lord Eadmund then addressed himself to Rhys. "Rhys, do you accept the title Lord Protector of Edenton and all the responsibilities that come with it?"

Rhys took a deep breath, "Only if the one true Lord help me."

Suddenly there was a murmur from the crowd, and someone pointed to the manor house. We all looked and saw Herlwin and Leof helping Carlyle, pale and weak, across the manor house lawn.

"Perhaps He has done so," Lord Eadmund said. A cheer went up for Carlyle and the monks. Eadmund waited till the monks stood next to them before continuing. "Let us end this proclamation of lordship with a prayer of blessing. Brother Carlyle?"

With Leof and Herlwin next to him, Carlyle stepped forward as Rhys knelt. Carlyle placed his left hand on Rhys' shoulder and his right on the lord's head and prayed,

> *"To He who is the Alpha and the Omega, the Beginning and the End, the One who makes all things new;*
>
> *Give grace to Your servant who carries the weight of Your glory, and may he bear well the image of the One True Lord.*
>
> *Your kingdom come, Your will be done in Edenton as it is heaven."*
>
> *Amen."*

And so it was that Rhys became Lord Protector of Edenton.

Unlike angels, all men die. But Carlyle lived long enough to be of great service to Lord Rhys. Rhys learned to rule over Edenton. He and Elene found that their mother had been taken to an abbey in Hibernia, and they sought her out which provided new adventures for them and kept their guardians busy.

Haelstrum and Zophar returned from Orion stronger than ever, but we did not have long to rejoice over Edenton together. For the day after they returned, Sargon found me in Edenton and gave me a message from Gabriel.

"Raiders from the north have been sacking villages near the sea coast. Devils have driven these raiders to destroy and kill. There are even rumors of a dragon appearing among them. Go to the sea coast with all speed and find a guardian named Trillium. He needs your help and if there is a dragon in the region, he will know where the dragon is."

"Who will watch over the Lord Guardian of Edenton?" I asked.

Sargon nodded at Zophar. "The one you trained yourself."

So I run. As water flows down a flood swollen river, I run. There are devils along the sea coast, so it is to there that I run. My breathing is not labored nor do I run in vain for I run in the power and the glory of my Creator, Captain of Angel Armies.

---

i Bradley, S.A.J., <u>Anglo Saxon Poetry</u>. London, J.M. Dent. Vermont, Charles E. Tuttle. Everyman, 2004. p 393.

# ABOUT THE AUTHOR

Jack Holbrook lives in Johnstown, Ohio with his wife, Betsy. They are blessed with four children; Judith, Katherine, Jonathan, and Peter. Jack is a fan of C.S. Lewis and J.R.R. Tolkien.

Jack is a graduate of Mount Vernon Nazarene University and The Ohio State University.